MW01258421

A TIME FOR REVENGE

The Black Revolution II

A Novel by

Richard Jeanty

RJ Publications, LLC

The characters and events in this book are fictitious. Any resemblance to actual persons, living or dead is purely coincidental.

RJ Publications, LLC

richjeanty@yahoo.com

www.rjpublications.com

ISBN: 978-1-939284-04-4

Printed in the United States of America

December 2023

1-2-3-4-5-6-7-8-9-10

ACKNOWLEDGEMENTS

I would like to thank the usual suspects; my family, close friends and all the people who have supported my writing career throughout the years. I especially want to give thanks to my two beautiful princesses, Rishanna and Richlyn and their mothers. Special love goes out to my mother, my father, my sister Kathy, my brother Alix, my cousin Alex, and my nephew Woodly, who have been great additions to my life, and all my nephews and nieces across the country and in Boston. Special shout out to my nephew Michael Jeanty in Atlanta and my very loving nephew Khalil DePasse. I would also like to thank Shawnee, Marley, Heather, Ginette, Alix, Widner, and all the great people I have met throughout my life, for their continuous support. My list of shout outs can be very long, but I have to take the time to shout out my lifelong friend, Los, aka Carlo Breneus. He's cut from a different cloth. A true friend indeed. Shout out to my homies, Kyle, Ray, Ralph (Bart), one of my main man and truest friend, Hensley, and all the people who consider me a friend that care about my well-being.

INTRODUCTION

When I first decided to write this book, I had no idea which direction it would take, but I knew that the book was important, and it needed to be written. It's been 10 long years since I've published a book, but I didn't want to rush the process, because my vision of the world has changed as I've gotten older. I've been lucky enough to travel around the world, and I've gotten exposed to the conditions of black people in every corner of the world. I'm truly disgusted with the hatred toward black people from the world, and the abject poverty conditions they have forced so many black people to embrace as a form of religion. Sometimes I wonder what it would take for black people to unify? We have been pushed to the brink of insanity, but yet, so many of us have managed to remain sane. By sane, I mean it in the most dysfunctional way, because too many of us are too flexible and too willing to bend to the will of white supremacy for survival's sake. Being able to adjust to any situation in order to overcome adversities, can be a gift and a curse. Our own resilience sometimes works against us as a people, because we are way too patient with white supremacy and too forgiving of white imperialism. We don't need any more testimonials from anybody in the black community, regarding their road to success, because we have always had to work twice as hard and overcome many obstacles in society to obtain success.

My purpose for this story is to infringe on the minds of the submissive, the obedient, the divisive, the self-hating Negro, and those black people who think personal success is a shield and armor from racism. As a matter of fact, your personal success is used against your own fellow black men and women who are failing every day because of systemic racism. They get to point to you as an achiever, in order to ostracize the ones who have fallen victim to the traps of racism. Most of the world stood together to voice their opinion on the conditions in Palestine and the way that the Palestinians have been marginalized for the past 75 years by the Zionists in Israel, but few people can see the prison without bars that black people have been subjected to in America, France, Great Britain, Brazil, and every part of the world. White imperialism is pervasive worldwide. Neo-colonialism is the new slavery without the chains and free labor. It's as if our natural gifts and talents have created a veil to our oppression, because people like Michael Jordan, Kobe, LeBron, Michael Jackson, Prince, Usher and so many others are praised and adored for their God-given prowess on the court and on stage, the sufferings of the majority of black people is ignored. The true reality for the majority of black people is oppression, exploitation, subjugation, and marginalization. To a certain degree, even the most talented and rich black people are exploited, marginalized, subjugated and oppressed. Kanye West can attest to that. Do black celebrities really have a voice that they can use to defend their black brethren? Most of us, no matter how talented we might be outside of sports and entertainment, have to fight hard to avoid the traps of racism and the trappings of white supremacy.

My job as a writer is to present you with the options that we have available to us, and for you to make an educated decision as to whether or not our unification as a race across the globe will serve us better as a group. Whether or not that message gets through to most black people who have read my books, that has yet to be determined. Only time will tell to see if the great awakening will take place in black communities all over the world. However, I do know that our survival on this planet is dependent on our unification as a people. For now, I'm just very proud of the African people in Niger, Burkina Faso, Gabon, and Mali.

THE UNIFICATION OF AFRICAN PEOPLE IS A MUST!

Given our position in the world, I don't see any other way to overcome white imperialism in the world without black people uniting for the greater good of the Alkebulan/African race. Our marginalization, subjugation, exploitation and oppression is layered to the point where black people all over the world are confused about their origin and where they belong in the world. Furthermore, too many of us confuse race with nationality. We tend to be more loyal to our nationality than to our African race. For the most part, if an African person was born and raised out of Africa, more than likely his nationality was forced upon him. To expound on this, I'll just say that my great great grandparents didn't make the decision to come to Virginia in 1619. My family's African roots ended when they captured the first member of my African tribe, kidnapped him or her, and brought them against their will to the United States to labor for free for a country that saw them as three fifths of a human being. As a matter of fact, it wasn't until 1868, when the 14th Amendment was ratified, that my ancestors were granted citizenship in this country. For over two hundred years, my ancestors lived in a country without an identity or nationality. How the hell did these uncivilized and unconscionable people come to the conclusion of calling black people three fifths of a human being, when they were civilized by the Moors?   Anyway, today we have more black people fighting to defend lands that their forefathers were forced to migrate to against their will, than they are willing to embrace their true heritage in honor of their ancestors.

I understand the disconnection to Africa has many variables, including the fact that all African countries turned their backs on their children after they were captured, and some Africans were used as middlemen during the slave trade. That's not really a history to embrace, but we cannot deny our African ancestry. The pride that we have developed for the nations where we were born is pride that is connected to the ignorance of our origin, and the fact that the terrorists of the world did everything in their power to make sure that black people could never again trace their connection to Africa. Slavery was the most organized crime humanity had ever seen. Taking away a race of people's language, custom, culture, religion, and last names is the epitome of subhuman concoction. They understood that in order to keep black people permanently in disarray and a confused state of being, they had to assign new language, religion and names to us. It's not a coincidence that most DNA companies offer the same data to most Africa-American and Caribbean people. They understand their data does not identify specific tribes in Africa, but only vague regions to suppress our curiosity about our origin. You can't do much with DNA information that leads you to Nigeria or Ghana, as there are many different tribes that existed then, and still exist today, that a person would have to figure out, in order to connect to the specific one. Slavery was well-orchestrated, and we continue to pay the price as black people, because we can't overcome our division and identity crisis. White supremacy is still winning, since we refuse to address our dysfunctions and correct all the wrongs that our forefathers endured, which has kept us in an enslave state up to this point.

Black folks are gonna have to do everything in their power to find common ground, in order for us to overcome their manipulating tactics of black people around the world. Meeting Candace has really opened my eyes to the depth of the division among black people. Though we are no longer on a slave ship, chained to one another, captured from different tribes, speaking different languages, and confused about our destination and future, but all the remnants of slavery are still present. We are more frustrated with each other than we are with our oppressor. We can find ways to get along with our oppressor faster than we can set aside our differences to achieve the goal of total freedom for ourselves around the world. My relationship with Candace has taught me many things, and educating my parents on our differences and commonalities as black people has been the most important lesson.

At this juncture, black people don't have a choice but to unite, or we'll face extinction as individuals and subgroups. History doesn't lie. The only black nation to have successfully fought against slavery was Haiti. The reason why Haiti was successful was because the leaders of the Haitian Revolution understood that "Unity is Strength" and they practiced it during the twelve-year war against the French, the Spanish and the British.

AMERICA'S ROLE
IN THE WORLD

Throughout my limited travels, I realized that America was built on propaganda, fear, injustice, illusion, deception, and pathology. I risked my life in Iraq simply because President Bush decided to invade Iraq to gain access to their lucrative oil, under the false pretense that Iraq held weapons of mass destruction. To this day, none have been found, not by us, or anybody, and President Bush was never imprisoned for giving the order to the US military to take the lives of millions of innocent Iraqis for no reason. As they have done everywhere they have invaded, US soldiers looted as many government palaces as possible and walked away with billions of dollars from the Iraqi coffers, and Saddam Hussein's personal stash. The US military is used as an imperialist reinforcement tool for white supremacy around the world, and these white imperialists usually face no consequences in international tribunals for their actions. As a former serviceman, I realized that my life and the lives of other servicemen are expandable, for as long as America wants to reinforce its supremacy around the world. The one percent is not risking the lives of their own children and family members in these wars. The casualties are often poor white people who have been brainwashed into believing their patriotism trumps the right of all other people around the world, and some black and brown slackers who are trying to figure out what to do with their lives. These poor white people and minority soldiers, who are often seeking better lives for themselves, tend to trust the military can be used as a conduit to a more prosperous life. It's a losing situation on both ends for all people who join. The aggression that America shows toward other countries around the world can only be curtailed when Americans start to open their eyes, and folks stop joining their military on the basis of patriotism and an escape from poverty. I'm saying this as a former Marine. The arrogance of America, or at least those elites who run America, will also be the reason for the downfall of America. We don't practice peace, nor do we believe in democracy. The propagandists who work for the US media are also responsible for the destruction of American society. Most Americans have a false sense of who they are because this country reinforces it through propaganda. It is delusional to believe that America is the leading country in the world, when America is 26.7 trillion dollars in debt without the resources to back the currency that they keep printing, and is not even top ten in any of the categories that would make this country one of the top countries in the world. America can only resort to aggressive tactics and forced invasions of other countries with great resources, in order to pay down this country's debt. Unfortunately, countries that are labeled "third-world," often have to pay the price for American arrogance. Most third-world countries have unlimited resources to sustain their people, but America, under the false pretense of philanthropy, usually act as saviors and donors handing out fake aid to these countries, so they can secure their natural resources on the back end. The over-exploitation of third world countries is the reason why these imperialist nations are able to use such a label on these countries.

I learned a long time ago from a childhood friend in Boston whose family was from Haiti that America has been sucking the life out of Haiti since their invasion of the country in 1915. It started when President Franklin D. Roosevelt decided to rewrite the constitution of the sovereign nation after the illegal invasion of Haiti. Germany had posed a threat to America's extortion and control of Haiti, so they decided to invade the country under false pretenses, and while there, they helped themselves to Haiti's national gold reserves, raided Haiti's national bank, and moved the loot to Citi Bank in America. Has America ever returned Haiti's gold or money? Hell no! There's never any consequence for white theft anywhere in the world. White people feel they can rob anybody whenever they want, or commit other egregious crimes against people and nations, because they set the judicial and moral standard for what's right in the world, and the world is supposed to accept their bullshit.

While the most common narrative in the US media about Haiti has always been "The poorest country in the western hemisphere," the US has been fully aware that Haiti possesses over 100 billion dollars in oil reserves, trillions of dollars in Iridium, and billions of dollars in gold, which they have been trying to position themselves to loot from Haiti ever since their invasion. America has wanted to take control of these resources for years, and Bill Clinton was nothing but an affront to accomplish that goal. The biggest scumbag to Haiti has been none other than Bill Clinton and his wife. They don't have any love for Haiti as they constantly and publicly proclaim. Their love is only material for Haiti's resources, but Haitians have opened their eyes a little too late to their game. Meanwhile, the people of Haiti have been suffering because of US intervention and manipulation of Haitian politics and their economy for the last century. Well, actually, since Haiti became an independent republic, which threatened the institution of slavery in America back then. We live in a filthy country full of chameleons who masquerade as the saviors of the world. The treatment of black people alone in this country should be enough of an indicator to the world that the American government is full of shit, and they should not be given access anywhere in the world where black and brown people live.

I find it interesting that black people in America have been fighting for reparations as descendants of slaves since the Emancipation Proclamation was signed, and no president has been willing to even have that discussion, not even the first black president, Barack Obama. However, these black fools and puppets who call themselves leaders across Africa and the Caribbean, still believe there's some goodwill that can come from America. America doesn't care about black people. Well, the goodwill that these puppets often believe in is usually discussed upfront, and it's always personal and beneficial to the puppets and their family directly. However, there have been a few puppets who tried to scrape up some crumbs on behalf of their people. America simply doesn't believe in goodwill. They simply believe in what they can get in return, and it's never an even exchange. The scale always has to tip in their favor. It will be noble when black leaders around the world start to wake up and see America for the enemy that she is, and always has been, against black people worldwide. Black progress in America seems to be a disservice to white supremacy, and white people will always see to it that black people are only in this country to serve them, no matter how rich they allow a black man to become because of his natural athletic, intellectual, or physical capabilities.

Even the richest black athlete in America is exploited by the system. Michael Jordan's name may be recognizable worldwide, but he collects less than 5% worth of royalties for a brand that was built on his name and likeness around the world. Sometimes, the thought of destabilizing racism alone is exhausting. I have so much work to do, in order to make sure my children don't fall into the trap of thinking America is the greatest country in the world. A great country doesn't incarcerate the highest amount of prisoners in the world. A great country should be on the top 10% list for the best education. A great country should not have a history of marginalizing a certain group because of race. A great country should not kill leaders around the world who don't support their interests. A great country should not be in debt for trillions of dollars. A great country should not allow racism to limit the opportunities of a certain race or group of people. A great country should make amends for their wrongs against the group of people that provided the free labor through slavery to make it great. A great country should encourage all its citizens to have a voice. Until all that happens, I will caution my children about this supposed great country called America.

The racist system in place has exploited black people to the tune of twenty-four trillion dollars of free labor during slavery, while continuously refusing to deliver on a promise of forty acres and a mule to right the wrongs of slavery. The US government owns 649 million acres of land, which can be allocated to the descendants of slaves as part of reparations, but instead, they like to financially support a country like Ukraine with billions of taxpayers' dollars. This country has a long way to go to show that it cares about its black citizen. If you're foolish enough to drink the Kool-Aid, you have chosen your poison. Black athletes and other professional and musically talented black people are usually isolated so that the government can point to the endless opportunities and possibilities that exist in America. However, they don't show the struggle of the 99.9% of black people who have to fight the system daily just to survive. Capitalism has always trumped racism, and the two have to coexist, in order for capitalism and racism to thrive. It's a contradiction in of itself, but that is the way of life in America that I'm learning. White people have used every denigrating racial epithet to refer to black people, and at the same time want black people to care for their children as nannies, housekeepers, drivers, and so on in their homes. They sure as hell couldn't pass on that free labor world to build their wealth. White people alone don't have enough talent to make sure the wheels of capitalism continue to spin, due to lack of effort, ingenuity, natural talent, and gift. They have to use manipulation against other people, in order for their ideal capitalism to work. There's no America without slavery, and there's no developed France, England, Spain, or Portugal without colonialism. And, if for some reason you decide to explore racism with the mindset of a sane individual, you might just become insane, because racism is a psychological disorder that is inexplicable at its core. The ignored fact that racism is a psychological disorder, is the very reason why white people will never stop being racist.

As much historical hatred that white people have harbored toward black people during slavery, and to this day around the world, it makes absolutely no sense why they even vacation in black countries. Racist white men who hate black people still want to have sex with black women through forced rapes. There's no rhyme or reason to their behavior, because it's just insanity and a psychological disorder. Furthermore, while some white folks didn't want to allow black people to drink from their water fountains or swim in their swimming pools, many of them allowed black women to breastfeed their children, cook their meals, and clean their houses. If that's not a psychological disorder, I don't know what is. Unless it's just plain idiocy, then I will never be able to make sense out of idiocy. I learned that a long time ago.

Sometimes I think about the lifetime condemnation of black people to poverty, inequality, harassment, injustice, and the inhumane indecency that so many of our black children have been subjected to around the world from birth, it makes me question whether or not I wanted to have kids of my own. Too often, black leaders are also complicit in the daunting task of condemning their own people to poverty and cruelty in their complacency to provide strong leadership. Since the Haitian Revolution, in which Jean-Jacques Dessalines fought hard to establish a free republic for black people in the West, no other black leader has made a strong effort to provide a sanctuary for black people anywhere in the world. Even during the 12-year battle against white imperialism, when Haiti had to face the British, the French and the Spanish, not one African country sent troops to help assist Haiti in their battles. The sanctity of blackness has been at the mercy of white imperialism dating all the way back to my ancestors who landed in America in slave ships. The blueprint to defeat white supremacy left behind by Jean-Jacques Dessalines, Toussaint L'Ouverture, and the rest of the revolutionaries in Haiti, has withered without proper use by any other fierce African leaders around the world. The imperialists have colluded to defeat Haiti in so many different ways, and in the process, have also managed to promote themselves using black puppets as leaders, by strategically placing them as heads of state in countries where they can ransack their resources and condemn the people to a life of poverty. They like to use the term "Third world" to dress up their cruelty against black and brown people, and unfortunately, few of us have stood up to the chameleon that these imperialists are.

The Third-World countries are pillaged, so these racists can call their habitats First World countries. In addition, they have used religion and missionaries as a weapon of mass destruction in all the black countries around the world as a pretext for improving the lives of black people. Will we ever wake up? I often question. My awakening journey only started to take shape after I joined the military, and even more, after I met Candace. After having been exposed to the cruelty we subject other people to around the world, I realized that imperialist colonizers are all about what they can take from the world to make life easier for the white folks in their own countries.

It has never been about creating a better world for anybody other than themselves.

I just hope that my children won't have to face the same struggles in their generation that I've had to face in mine. The biggest mistake black people could've made was to integrate with these devils. I really don't give a shit about their integration. It doesn't benefit me in any way. There isn't one good thing integration has done for black people born during my era; the school system has worsened, it has allowed white people to take control of businesses that were once owned and run by black people, it has given them access to properties and communities that were once predominantly black-owned, and ran by black people for the benefit of the black family and the black community at large. In addition, these culture vultures believe the police are their personal bodyguards, so they use them to reinforce white supremacy and their racism at will. I'm tired of all these "Karens" everywhere I go. It's a shame that we have to create different stigmas for racism almost every decade. I want to raise my kids in a world where they won't be harassed by cops, just because of the color of their skin. Sometimes I question whether or not white folks believe in humanity at all, because their history of hatred dates back to civilization, and there's a new generation of hateful white people born every day, it seems. They can't let go of their hatred, even after four hundred years of forcing black people to live among them and forcing them to work for free. How has a group of people function on hatred for so long? That's probably a question that my grandchildren will still probably be asking one hundred years from now.

A WELL-DESIGNED
SLAVERY SYSTEM

I'm not that old, but I'm old enough to understand that everything happens for a reason, and that there are no coincidences. Candace and I were meant to connect the way we did. Life's lessons come at us in different ways, and sometimes they challenge us to challenge the normalcy that is before us with obscured eyes. All the people in America, whether black, white, brown, or yellow, it doesn't matter, they are here purposefully, and it is part of their destiny, even those people who risked their lives on small rafts over deadly seas to get here. Sometimes we think we can dictate our own destiny, but that's not always the case. There's a well-oiled machine in place called racism that sometimes directs our destiny unbeknownst to us. America thrives on imperialism. It's their way of controlling the world, and it's how they dictate the world's economy, wars, and everything else that affects life on Earth. As I've gotten older, I've learned to peel the layers, so that I'm not easily fooled by the propaganda set in place to keep me in a stupor that benefits a certain group and class of people. Most of the time, people come into our lives to enlighten us and to shape our lives in a direction that is necessary for survival, whether negative or positive. My commitment to Candace not only defines who I am as a man, but also my dedication to be a good father and husband to my future children and her. She's been my rock, and she has opened my eyes to so many things that I wasn't privy to. I'm grateful for having met her, and she's the reason that I can now express my reservations about America as a country and its timeless and endless mission to keep black people in a cycle of poverty and second-class citizen status.

My desire to be great for Candace has also forced me to scrutinize things that I wouldn't have otherwise scrutinized or analyzed prior to meeting her. I've always been a cerebral guy, but my intellectual curiosity was limited to the tech world. I never really ventured out to history, the arts or anything else that would complete the package of the individual that I aim to be. Candace sort of gave me that sense of purpose. After meeting her family and hearing the stories about their struggles, I decided to dig deeper into the history of my own family and this country, as it relates to the hierarchy they've established in the world. While America claims to be the leader of the world, and a place that offers opportunity to all, it's also a place where they have conveniently and creatively established innovative tactics to keep black and immigrant people in a servitude position to white people. As a matter of fact, slavery never really ended in this country. It has been masqueraded and paraded in front of the world inconspicuously, but few people have closely examined the deceptions. Because we don't see shackles and chains around our arms and ankles anymore, and nobody is bound or gagged on some plantation that is obvious to the eyes, we've proclaimed that slavery had seen its end. Even after the Emancipation Proclamation was signed, many plantation owners kept the news from the people they enslaved. Many of our ancestors worked those fields for decades before they learned that slavery had been abolished. The constitutional claim, "We hold these truths to be self-evident, that all men are created equal, that they are endowed by their Creator with certain unalienable Rights, that among these are Life, Liberty, and the pursuit of Happiness" is quite the contrary to black people in America. The constitution was written by racists who had to be coerced into practicing the false narratives they were preaching to the world. Still, their constitution is only theory, even today.

A closer examination of the practice of slavery would reveal that slavery continues to thrive right before our eyes and under our noses like fresh roses blooming in the spring. And America will never do anything to change that. It serves America well that slavery is improved and has taken a different shape, where a certain sector of society can point fingers at a certain group to condemn them without feeling any guilt. You see, when something is not obvious to the eyes and people can't point directly to it to say, "That's the problem," we tend to be ambivalent. Most people ignore ambivalence, because it's just an obscure conflict, and not necessarily a reality that needs immediate attention.

My awakening journey led me to question many things, and research everything, including the Emancipation Proclamation, its purpose, and what they had set in place to help black people adjust to their newfound "freedom." The more I dug into this subject, the more I realized that slavery never ended in America, and that the government just made it a lot more complex for people to figure out. While Abraham Lincoln emerged a hero to many black people who were too illiterate to understand their reality, and many liberals who were looking for an opening to present themselves as saviors and friends of the Negro, the underlying factor remains, Lincoln was a racist and he was in no way enthusiastic about ending slavery. Lincoln's own words about black people openly confirmed his racist views, as it related to the equality of black people to white people. The signing of the Emancipation Proclamation by President Abraham Lincoln offered absolutely no hope for the former black slaves in America. As a matter of fact, it further empowered slave owners at the time, and placed the culpability of servitude squarely on the shoulders of black people who had nowhere to go after the country announced they were free. Free to do what exactly? Where were black people moving to? How were they going to feed themselves? How would they earn a living? Where would they sleep? When a child is kicked out of a parent's house, that child has to learn to survive on his/her own, right? The only other choice is for that child to make the decision to obey his parents, in order for him/her to continue to live in his/her parents' house. That was the deal that black people were left with after the Emancipation Proclamation was signed. It was genius on the part of Lincoln at the time, but why did Lincoln seek the assistance of black people during the Civil War? At that point in my life, I was questioning everything, and if it didn't make sense, I theorized my own answer, or at least examined the system or people that benefited the most from the decision to free the slaves.

The basic definition of freedom is unrestricted use or access, freedom of movement, possession of civil rights, the condition of being free, political independence, and a myriad of other explanations, none of which applied to black people at the time. First of all, black folks didn't enjoy the benefits of political independence, and neither did they have the freedom of movement, possession of civil rights, or unrestricted use or access. As a matter of fact, black people became more restricted without access than ever. Before the Emancipation Proclamation was signed, the slave owners could at the very least, treat their grown slaves like children, by handing them a note to say they were permitted to go to the store to run errands on their behalf. After Abe Lincoln signed the Emancipation Proclamation, Congress soon followed up with federal vagrancy laws that prevented black people from being in the streets, without having an actual place they could call home. Those vagrancy laws also allowed the newly freedmen to be arrested and taken to jail, where they were again enslaved, according to the laws on the books which made it legal for prisoners to be enslaved. Those same prisoners could be outsourced on consignment to their former slave owners for a fee paid to the government. White imperialism is tricky, and it takes a lot of patience to try to understand their conning tactics, and how they have always managed to undermine black people.

Let's cut the shit out, because we know that white history is filled with lies. Let's explore the real reason why Lincoln decided to allow black soldiers to join the Union Army during the Civil War in the first place. The whole bullshit narrative about black people weren't fit to serve in the US military is bullshit. White people in America were afraid that black people would one day rise and revolt like the Haitians did against the French, British, and Spanish in Hispaniola. There had been many rebellions in the United States that were inspired by the Haitian Revolution. The literate black people, such as Frederick Douglass, who had read about the Haitian Revolution, were starting to educate other black people and inspire them to stand up for themselves. Lincoln understood the imminent threat, but he wanted to make sure that white people would still be in control. The promise of 40 acres and a mule to encourage black people to join the Union side of the war was just a ploy. Lincoln's true intention was to return black folks to Liberia, a country founded by former American slaves in Africa. In addition, America had conspired with France and Britain to return slavery to Haiti 50 years after the Haitian liberation war against European tyranny. Lincoln knew the threat well because the Haitian Revolution helped America secure the Louisiana Purchase, which included many other states besides Louisiana. Over 500 Haitian soldiers had helped America fight against the British during the Revolutionary War at the Battle of Savannah in 1779, almost a century before the Emancipation Proclamation was signed. White people were well aware that black people were valiant and could potentially defeat them in battle anywhere in the world. The Haitian Revolution instilled fear in all the colonizers around the world. The United States' history books reflect a history of black people that started with slavery, and they have purposely omitted from their texts the uprisings that took place across the country by black people in bondage, which were inspired by the Haitian Revolution. No one can develop a strong sense of being without understanding their connection to greatness. The Haitian Revolution was not about Haiti alone, it was a revolution to end slavery worldwide, and it did exactly that in the New World. Without the Haitian Revolution, slavery would have lingered in America probably until the end of time. Still, it took America and the other European colonizers over fifty years to recognize Haiti as the first black republic, where slavery was eradicated. As a condition to be recognized as a free republic, America colluded with France and Britain to force the Haitian government to pay 112 million Francs to France as restitution to the slave owners in the former colony. America and its imperialist allies vowed to place embargoes against the Haitian government to prevent them from trading with other countries. When people hear about the Haitian Revolution, most of the time, they think only slaves who were transported to Haiti fought in those battles. That couldn't be further from the truth. Hispaniola had become an island known for breaking down the toughest rebellious slaves, and many other slaves from the surrounding islands in the Caribbean who rebelled against their masters were sent to Haiti for harsher discipline and punishment. When a group of rebels get together, they're going to rebel. The slaves in Haiti decided to put aside their differences to revolt against bondage as one unified group. The slave owners in Haiti were known as the harshest disciplinarian, and a lot of the rebellious slaves were not going to be broken into submission. Instead of accepting the inhumane treatment at the hands of these white devils, the rebels, led by General Jean-Jacques Dessalines who was born in Grande Riviere Du Nord in Haiti, Toussaint L'Ouverture who was born in Cap Haitien, Dutty Boukman who had been shipped from Jamaica, but was born in Senegambia (Senegal/Gambia) and George Biassou who was born in Cap Haitien, along with Henri Christophe who was born in Grenada, who served as a drummer boy for the US army in the Battle of Savannah to help free Georgia, along with 500 other Haitian soldiers who were sent by the French government to help assist the United States in their Revolutionary war against the British, and Alexandre Petion who was a mulatto, born in Haiti to a black mother and a white father who had been trained by the military school in France, decided they were going to fight for their freedom or died trying. Black people have always been valiant.

After the assassination of Lincoln, many states moved swiftly to enforce the vagrancy laws that would further enslave black people through incarceration, and their penal system would continue the practice of slavery as a result, and with the understanding that black people had no right and representation to fight these laws. These laws forced many newly freed people to accept their positions as slaves voluntarily, as many of them had no choice but to stay with their masters to avoid frivolous incarceration on the street. Today, the same law is referred to as loitering, and it is mostly enforced against black people in their own black community. The criminalization of black people in America is rooted in slavery in every aspect. Even after America supposedly emancipated black people from slavery, America continued to covertly benefit from slave labor in so many different ways through their newly enacted laws. They continued the practice of free labor by leasing the prison chain gangs to plantation owners for lower fees. Nowadays, corporations get to pay prisoners pennies on the dollar, by signing long-term leases for prison labor with private prison owners. These private prison owners in their contracts with state and federal prison officials require that their prisons maintain a full capacity of prisoners at all times, which reinforces the prison industrial complex. The cycle of slavery has taken a new shape and form in modern-day America. The former slave patrols are now called law enforcement, laced in new Klan outfits that they refer to as blue uniforms, and they get to carry badges as they did when they were part of the slave patrol, and continue to murder black people indiscriminately, while hiding behind their own racist code of ethics called "The Blue Code Of Silence. All the major urban cities around America are now using the police to chase black men around, sometimes for no reason at all other than profiling, and criminalizing them at a higher rate than any other group over trivial bullshit to keep the private prisons filled to capacity, to satisfy their thirst for racism and the people investing in their private prisons. Private prisons have yielded high returns for private investors, and legislation has been enacted by senators and signed by presidents to ensure the new wheels of slavery continue to be oiled right before our very eyes. Prison lobbyists are some of the biggest donors to the campaigns of senators, congress members, and State Representatives. Systemic racism is practiced with a smokescreen, and it's very difficult to uncover and decipher, because the media also plays a major role in continuing the marginalization and subjugation of black people. It takes critical thinking to fairly assess a system that has worked to perfection against black people for centuries now. Digging through all that history was painful and exhausting. However, I'm glad that I went through it, because it gives me a better sense of who I am, where I came from, and how I need to move in society.

MEETING THE PARENTS

Before I met Candace's parents, she warned me of their possible prejudice toward African-Americans, which was influenced by the stereotypes, propaganda, and false narratives they often saw and heard on television about black people, to keep the division between African-Americans and black immigrants. I anticipated a little of their close-mindedness, but I didn't set out to prove anything to them. I want them to see me and judge me as an individual. Still, I wanted to try to understand the root of their biased way of thinking, as it related to African-Americans. Why were they so influenced by the media, and what was the reason behind it? From talking to Candace, it was very clear to me that the picture the media paints of black people in this country doesn't just influence the minds of white people, but also affects the thinking of foreign black people who also experience racism themselves at the hands of white people daily in this country. I want to know how they're able to compartmentalize the racism they face, and how it's different from the racism I face as an African-American man. "Most black foreigners don't understand that African-Americans fought during the Civil Rights Movement to open doors for them, so they are able to migrate to this country as free citizens with unalienable rights. The hard work and dedication of African-Americans toward civil rights and justice offers every benefit that any black immigrant is able to enjoy here in America. It was because of the sweat, suffering, and tears of the African-Americans who fought before they arrived here that they're able to call this country home," Candace open-mindedly said to me. She understood this, but I imagined her parents might've been blinded a little by "white savior syndrome," because they failed to make the correlation between being forced to flee their homeland because of manipulation and undermining of their government by the United States, and the imposition of a puppet to ensure US interest is a priority in Haiti, while in search of a better life in America. For some reason, a lot of immigrants seem to think that most African-Americans don't maximize their restricted and limited opportunities here, without taking the time to look at the entire state of black people in this country, in order to better understand the structural racism in place and the plight of African-Americans, according to what Candace has mentioned about her own experience with other immigrants who usually feel comfortable enough to speak freely and openly around her because her parents are immigrants.

Oftentimes when two cultures meet, there might be some disagreements that need to be sorted out, but the problems arise when people start to believe their own prejudice that African-Americans and other black people are homogenous, and our black skin should be enough to connect all of us. That couldn't be farther from the truth. There are many different types of black cultures throughout the world, and none of them are alike. Colonialism has affected black people in so many different ways, but African-Americans and Afro-Brazilians are affected in the worst way. They are the only two groups of people who were enslaved and forced to live among their enslavers in the greatest numbers in concentrated areas with higher number of whites. In addition, a fear of revolt always loomed over the heads of the slave owners, which forced them to act inhumanely and harshly toward the slaves who lived on their plantation. Morally, they all understood that slavery was illegal and immoral, but they were willing to take all the risks, for as long as their governments chose to protect them against the illegal act of slavery. I learned many things about Caribbean culture from Candace, but more importantly, I learned the difference between Haitians and other Caribbean folks. Every Caribbean country has a culture of its own with different influences from its former colonizers. Some of these influences include French, English, Dutch, Spanish, or a mixture of these. St. Marten is a small island divided between the French and the Dutch. The colonizers would fight one another for the right to colonize and control the different islands in the Caribbean, and each time an island was taken over by the French or the British, the language and culture shifted. Another great example of that is the dual languages spoken in St. Lucia and Dominica. Both countries have people who speak a Creole patois that is derived from a mixture of French and English because the islands were fought over and colonized by both, the French and the British. The older folks in Trinidad and Grenada all spoke a Creole language that derived from French at one point in time, because the French had control over those islands before the British fought them and took them over. The slaves from Africa were brought together from different regions of Africa, so the language barrier among them forced them to create their own languages, every time they were exploited by new colonizers. The different variations of French and English patois spoken and created by different Caribbean islanders, is evidence of the ingenuity of African people.

The colonizers have never had to assimilate into the culture of the people they exploited. However, the Africans were not only forced to learn new languages, they had to assimilate into the new cultures, and religions forced upon them. And they thought Africans were less smart and less human than them? The fucking nerve! The subcultures created by Africans in the Diaspora represents the potpourri that is blackness, and the resilience to conform to situations that black people have demonstrated since the beginning of time, in order to survive this long. We are greater and they've always known it. The history lessons I received from Candace as an Afri-can-American about Caribbean culture are invaluable. Her dad did a great job teaching her about her own culture, as well as the culture of other Caribbean people.

In order to have a clearer picture of Candace's family back-ground and culture, I decided to spend Thanksgiving with them after Candace and I became engaged. I knew she would eventually become my wife, so meeting her parents was unavoidable. I jumped at the opportunity to go home with her. Poor Candace, she tried to prep me as much as possible about how to address her parents and behave around them, so that we could have their blessing, but I wasn't going to change the man that I was, just to please her par-ents. My parents didn't raise me to be disrespectful in any way, so that was not going to be an issue. I had home training, and I wanted to make sure Candace's parents knew that I was a great man and good enough for their daughter. She held on to my hand tightly during the entire flight to New York from Atlanta, and she smiled, every time we locked eyes while reaching over to give me a reassur-ing kiss. She was trying to overcome her own nervousness for the man she loves. A woman like her deserved the world, and I intended on giving it to her the best way that I could.

We finally landed at LaGuardia airport on the Tuesday before Thanksgiving. Candace seemed nervous and eager at the same time. She hadn't seen her parents in almost a year, and she was now bringing home a fiancée for them to meet. I wasn't completely sure what Candace had told her parents about me, and I was confident it was all positive. My nervousness never subsided as we walked toward the baggage claim area to pick up her luggage. I packed light, and only had a carry-on for the five days that we had planned on being in New York, but Candace was a different story. It seemed like she'd packed the entire apartment in her two suitcases, a carry-on that she boarded the plane with, and another one she checked in. We were standing around waiting for her checked-in luggage when this petite, but strong looking brown-skinned woman, casually dressed in a skirt, a sweater, and a jacket, ran up on her and wrapped her arms around her in a long hug. I didn't have time to react to the situation, but I soon realized the woman was her mother, because Candace had a big Kool-Aid smile on her face when she turned around to see, and then heard her mom's thick Haitian accent, an accent I hadn't heard from anyone since I left Boston. Most people in the south confuse every Caribbean accent as a Jamaican accent, without realizing the different variations of accents that exist in the Caribbean. "Look at you," her mother said after stepping back to take a good look at her daughter. "You look good, too," Candace told her mother, before enveloping herself in a hug again. "This is my boyfriend, I mean, my fiancée, Kane," Candace told her mom, as she pointed toward me. "Nice to meet you, ma'am," I said, after extending my hand to shake hers. "No, we don't shake hands in this family. You're gonna be my son-in-law, we hug. I'm Marjorie.

Nice to meet you," her mom said, while hugging me. "He's handsome just like your father," her mother whispered to her. "Mommy, don't start. He can hear us, you know?" she told her mom. "Your dad is outside waiting in the car. He can't wait to see you. All he's been talking about is seeing his princess," her mom told her. "I can't wait to see him either. I miss Daddy," she told her mom. Candace's suitcase finally came down on the belt. I grabbed her suitcase, along with mine, and walked toward the moment of truth. It seemed like I had already passed the test with mom, so it was her dad who was outside waiting in the car that I was worried about now.

The shiny and clean looking Toyota 4 Runner was idling in front of the sliding doors when we set foot outside the airport. Her dad was anxiously waiting and looking out for Candace. The minute he laid eyes on her, he jumped out of the car and started running toward her for a hug. "My baby," he said in what sounded like a French and Caribbean accent mix, as he picked her up from the ground. Her father was a little taller than I expected. He was a couple of inches taller than me, and he dressed like he was going to a meeting, with a button-down shirt, slacks, shoes, and a sport coat. Her dad was also quite youthful looking for his age, and well-groomed. "Hi Daddy," Candace said while hugging her dad as if she were a 5-year old girl, with a big ass smile on her face. She gave him a long hug that was broken by the sound of a whistle blown by a traffic cop, to make sure her dad moved his car quickly. "Let me get your bags," he said, as he pressed the button to open the lift gate in the back of his SUV. I walked toward the car, and placed Candace's suitcase in the trunk, along with mine. "Thank you very much," her father said while handing me a couple of dollars. He thought I was a skycap for some reason. "Daddy, what are you doing?" Candace asked after she saw this attempt to hand me money. "What do you mean? I'm giving him a tip for carrying your bags," her father said. "Daddy, don't be silly. This is my fiancée, Kane. I told you I was bringing him home for Thanksgiving," she told her dad through a silly laugh. "Oh, I'm sorry. This is the young man who stole my daughter's heart?" he asked. "How're you doing, sir? My name is Kane," I said with my hand extended, waiting to shake his. "Did my daughter tell you that I once skinned a man alive in Haiti?" he said sounding serious in a joking way. There was no fear in my heart, so I chuckled at his statement. He finally shook my hand and said, "Well, I guess I have no choice but to get to know you, since you want to marry my daughter. However, before I agree to do all that, baby, let me see that ring," he said, so everyone could hear. Candace extended her hand to show her dad the ring. "It's good. I guess you qualify to be my son-in-law after all. We'll find out more about you in the next few days," he said. Her dad was trying to be funny, and I thought it was cool. I didn't mind. "Sir, I really would like to make it official by asking you for your daughter's hand in marriage," I said after hopping in the car. "The only thing that matters to me is my baby's happiness. As long as she's happy with you, you're okay with me, and you have my approval and blessing. From where I'm stand-ing, she seems pretty happy. And it's not like y'all ain't gonna marry if I said no, anyway," he said while laughing, and then her mother chimed, "I haven't approved of anything yet. We still have to get to know this young man," her mother said with a serious tone. I was a little uneasy, but Candace grabbed my hand to reassure me that her mom will come along eventually. I thought I had moms in the bag, but it was her dad who was the easier parent to persuade. I had my work cut out for me, because her mom was definitely tougher than her dad.

The ride to Elmont, New York, was about forty-five minutes from LaGuardia airport with all the traffic. Candace and I were sit-ting in the back seat. I whispered in her ear, "You just messed up our lunch money. I was gonna keep that tip from your dad." She laughed and said, "You're so crazy." Candace had a way of making me feel self-assured and confident, and "You're so crazy" was one of my favorite reassuring sentences from her. That was her way of letting me know how much she loved me. The family tried as much as they could to catch up, while we were in the car. Candace's mom was especially chatty, while her dad was more reserved and quiet. I didn't speak unless I was spoken to, and Candace kept rubbing my arm and hands to take away my nervousness. The exchanges were both in English and Haitian Creole, but Candace made it a point to always speak in English in my presence, so I could have an idea of what was being said. It was obvious that her parents were more comfortable speaking in their native tongue, and I had no problem with that. "So, have you guys decided if you're going to have the wedding in New York or Atlanta?" Marjorie asked. However, before Candace and I could even answer, she followed up with another question, "Kane, is your family from Atlanta?" "No, my family's actually from Boston. I don't really have family in Atlanta," I responded. "Oh, I have cousins and other family members in Boston. I go to Boston with my husband all the time. Where in Boston are you from?' she asked. "I grew up in Dorchester, right off Morton Street," I told her. "I know Dorchester. Some of my family members live in Dorchester. That's good," she said. Candace was sitting there quietly and listening to the exchange between me and her mom. Her mom did a 180 without even realizing it. She was interested in our life together. Out of the blue, her dad finally said something, "Kane, did you go to college?" I wasn't sure where he was going with that, but I responded by reminding him that Candace and I met on our college campus, and we both attended the same school. I also told him that I was in the military, but he wasn't a fan of the US military. "No black man belongs in the US military. The government doesn't respect black people, not even black veterans. They use you guys to invade places like my country, and make sure we stay in misery forever," he said. "I have never been to Haiti, sir," I told him. "Well, I'm not talking about you personally, but the government sends American soldiers all over the world to disrupt people's lives in their own country. And they want to control people all over the world. A lot of people like myself, had to flee my home country because of the US government's meddling into our politics and way of life. They don't want us to breathe. White people treat black people like Eric Garner and George Floyd all over the world. They want to choke us to death, in a figurative and literal way at the same time" he said. Her father was deep. I didn't anticipate this type of conversation so soon after meeting him, but to a certain degree, he was right. I was just an expendable body to the US government, and I received orders from them to bring their wrath upon innocent people all over the world. Most of the time, a lot of us in the military didn't even know what we were fighting for, or the reason we were sent to these foreign countries to defend America's democracy. Come to think of it, I faced more racism at home after I got out of the military than I did overseas from the people we invaded. This conversation was actually right up my alley. "I might've been a soldier in the white man's army, but there were circumstances that brought me there, and I had a goal that I wanted to achieve. I wasn't just any soldier," I said to him. "That's good to know. You seem like a smart young man. I hope I raised my daughter well enough to make smart decisions when it comes to a man. So far, I like you. It can only go up from there. We'll see in a couple of days. As long as you keep my daughter smiling, I'm always going to like you. Being a soldier doesn't scare me either. I will kick your ass, if you hurt my daughter, too," he said while laughing.

Things started off pretty well at Candace's parents' home. I was set up in the guest room. Her mom made breakfast and dinner pretty much every day that I was there, and it seemed to be a regular practice whenever she had time to cook before she went to work, and when she got home after work. I was only there for a couple of days, so it's hard to say definitively. I don't know where she got that energy, but that woman was strong. Of course, her father and I bonded on a different level. I got to learn about his political views and how growing up under a dictatorship in Haiti shaped his vision as a man. In addition, we also talked about religion and the whitewashing of it all, and the brainwashing of black people during slavery to reinforce a white savior in Jesus. Mr. Joseph believes, without the white man's religion black people would be unified, and a lot stronger around the world. "So many black people are living for a heaven in the sky created by white people that they are failing to live their lives while on earth. Life after death in some fictitious heaven is a myth. It's a myth that white people created that they don't even follow themselves. They rob, extort and murder people around the world daily. So the 10 commandments in the bible don't apply to them? Imagine allowing a group of people the capacity to psychologically disrobe an entire race of their belief system, culture, heritage, language, and spirituality, which is the biggest strength any human can possess, and for an entire continent to adapt to and adopt those values as their own? This renders anybody a trained puppy who will forever look to his owner for guidance,"

38

Mr. Joseph told me. I had never thought about it that way. It took a moment of reflection for me to realize the weight of his truth. Mr. Joseph didn't believe in any of that white Jesus stuff. He was his own man and researched his lineage back to Africa and the African spirituality that helped his countrymen gain independence from the French. He wasn't ashamed or apologetic about believing in African Vodou. His parents had raised him that way. Mr. Joseph schooled me on many things about African spirituality and Haitian Vodou, which originated from the Fon people under the Dahomey kingdom, which is modern day Benin in Africa, where most people of Haitian descent were stolen from, and forced into slavery in Haiti. One of the main reasons why Haiti became the only country to fight for its independence is because of their lineage to the Fon people who were a united group of fearless and military skilled people who had fought many wars to defend the Dahomey Kingdom. Some of those people were also taken to Jamaica and other islands in the Caribbean. Because of the language barrier among the slaves, they could not band together sooner to force a revolt, as many of them were from different tribes and spoke different languages after they were captured into slavery. After they managed to create their own language, modern-day Haitian Creole, which derives from the language of their captors, the French, and many other variations of it throughout the Caribbean islands from the British, Spanish, and Dutch colonizers, these Africans became forever loyal to their drop-off locations, the custom of their masters, their masters and their new religion, except for the Haitians. A few years after arriving on the island of Hispaniola, which is now modern day Haiti and the Dominican Republic, the slaves got together and called on their African God to protect them against their enslavers during a ceremony that took place at Bwa Kayiman, which was led by another slave who was shipped to Haiti by way of Jamaica called, Dutty Bookman. Some of the things her father was telling me, I had already researched for myself, in case the topic came up in conversation. I was able to hold my own about The Haitian Revolution, and her dad seemed impressed with my knowledge about Haiti. "I see you have done your homework on Haitian culture. You must truly love my daughter. I respect that," he said. "The Haitian revolution is not discussed much in white academia, because it would've emboldened black folks around the world with bravery and valor that would have forced white people to flee back to Europe. Black people had the valor to fight, but because of language barriers, they lacked the organization in America and the Caribbean. The Haitians managed to outsmart their white captors under the leadership of Toussaint L'Ouverture and his ruthless and fearless general, Jean-Jacques Dessalines," I told him, as if I were an historian. Mr. Joseph was an interesting and educated man. He made sure he tried my knowledge of his culture, sizing me up to make sure I was good enough for his daughter. Some of the topics we discussed during the few days at his house were never brought up by Candace during our discussions in the span of time that I'd known her. Candace was always very quiet but very knowledgeable about the rich history of her parents' country and the fact that Dessalines, one of the founders of the Haitian revolution, also brought the dignity of the African monarchy to Haiti when he proclaimed himself emperor of Haiti. In addition, I also learned from her that Dessalines made it his mission to try to free every black person who was kidnapped into slavery on the way to America from Africa. He often offered to buy their freedom, and when that wasn't possible, he would encourage the Haitian pirates to seize the ships and free the slaves. Any black person who escaped slavery and was able to reach Haitian soil was considered a free man or woman. As a nation, Haiti posed a huge threat to the slave trade in America and the rest of the Caribbean region.

While Candace's mom didn't say much about history and religion, she definitely supported her husband and believed African spirituality is much stronger than any Christian religion. The hierarchy in the family was obvious. There was no reason to question who the head of the household was, or the leader of the family. Mrs. Joseph was not submissive by any means, however, she understood her role as a wife, queen, and mother, and allowed her husband to be the king of his castle, while he treated her as his queen. It was a good situation all around. And I loved every minute of my stay with the family. Though not as politically astute as her husband, Mrs. Joseph, however, took the time to explain to me how the slaves were forbidden from practicing their own religion, were beaten by their white captors, and forced to learn a special bible specifically written and created to reinforce obedience, submission, docility, and an enslaved mind. In Haiti, though, the slaves were a different breed. They understood so much more about nature, the trails in the mountains, natural medicine, natural poison, and were overall a lot smarter than their white oppressors.

Other than the fact that these ships dropped off our ancestors at different locations once they arrived in the West, we are all the same people from Africa, and we need to remember that. We should never allow white people to separate us as Africans. No African person originated from Haiti, Jamaica, Trinidad, Brazil, America, or any of the locations where they were enslaved. All black people originated from Africa, and we must remember that. Africa is the unifier for all of us," he told me. Mr. Joseph had a point. Most of us are walking around calling ourselves American, Haitian, Jamaican, Cuban, Brazilian and so on, without realizing our bloodline came from the same continent. We are one people, and the sooner we unify under that umbrella, the better off we will be collectively as the African race. Mr. Joseph was definitely a unifier, and I saw something in him that I had never seen in any black man that I had ever met before in my life. He was self-assured, confident, and knowledgeable.

WHEN NOSTALGIA KICKED IN

Since we were in New York and only a four-hour drive from Boston, I decided maybe it was time for me to go home and visit my parents. I hadn't seen them in a while, and being around Candace's family rubbed off on me in the most positive way, and it made me want to see my own parents. I brought up the idea to Candace for us to drive to Boston to see my parents, and she had no problem with it. Besides, she needed to meet my parents, anyway. "I think it'll be great for you to go home and spend a couple of days with your parents. We don't leave til Sunday night, so you have plenty of time to come back and catch our flight," she said, without fully understanding that I wanted to take her home with me to meet my parents as well. "Babe, I wasn't planning to go home alone. I want you to come along with me. Since I've met your parents, it's only fair that you meet mine," I said to her. She had to think about it for a minute. "Babe, I didn't bring anything to wear. I can't just show up at your parents' house looking any old way. You have to warn a sister," she said with apprehension in her tone. "Babe, all you need is to be yourself. The same clothes you brought to wear around your parents are good enough to wear around my parents. They're gonna love you, because I love you. I'm sure of it," I assured her. "Since you insist, I'll see what I can do to make my baby happy," she said jokingly. She didn't have to say anymore. I knew she was coming with me.

After agreeing to go to Boston with me, I needed to make a reservation to pick up a rental car from the airport. Since we were flying out of LaGuardia back to Atlanta, I asked Candace to see if her dad could take us to the airport in the morning to pick up a car from the rental center. I used my phone to make the reservation for a small SUV from Hertz. After dinner that night, the family played dominoes and chatted about everything. Sometimes they spoke English and other times they spoke their native tongue, which was natural to them. I didn't mind. I wanted Candace to be comfortable being herself around her family. I also picked up a few words, in the process. "Sak pase" is one of the most common and popular greetings, so I picked that up right away. "Nap boule" is the response to that greeting, so I also picked that up. Every now and then Candace would teach me a word or two in Creole, but I don't always remember all of them. I watched how they played dominoes and learned that it's no different than the way we play, except for a few minor things like playing on four sides of a spinner. Haitians don't even acknowledge a spinner, and they don't score points. Haitians play until the first person who's able to put down his last domino or last piece, to match either ends of the dominoes on the table, is the winner. I learned while watching the three of them play, and after about four games, I was able to join them, to play their way. Now, I'm pretty decent at playing Haitian domino. It was all part of the meet and greet during the time I spent at her parents' house. They were very welcoming and kind to me. I could really see that family growing on me in the most positive way.

Hanging around Candace's family on Thanksgiving brought on a nostalgic feeling I hadn't felt in a while. Even though they didn't "celebrate" Thanksgiving, because Mr. Joseph is probably the most rebellious, knowledgeable, and proud man that I have ever met, we did have a great dinner consisting of traditional Haitian food. Mrs. Joseph cooked rice and beans, macaroni and cheese, the Haitian way, legume, which is a potpourri of vegetables cabbage, eggplants, chayote, carrots, watercress, and spinach, cooked with Haitian spices, beef and crab. Mr. Joseph cautioned why his family didn't celebrate Thanksgiving. Even though assimilation has forced a lot of immigrant families to join in the festivities of Thanksgiving, Mr. Joseph had researched the holiday and decided his family would never participate in the celebration of the annihilation of the Native Americans. In addition, he also mentioned that he had never heard of Thanksgiving until he moved to America. After eating this wonderful dinner cooked by his wife with the assistance of Candace in the kitchen, I wondered how my parents were doing, and if it was a good thing to surprise them. That family moment I shared with my future wife and her family was the same experience I wanted her to have with my own family. My parents usually hold a traditional annual Thanksgiving dinner at the house, and sometimes family would come from out of town to stay with them. While the idea of surprising them sounded good, I knew it wasn't practical. I decided it was best to call them and let them know I was coming. My mother was excited to learn that I was coming, but she was sad at the same time, because I had missed the actual Thanksgiving festivities with my family. It was a bittersweet situation. I did tell her that I had a surprise, but I didn't mention what it was. My dad was his usual self on the phone. We talked briefly and he looked forward to seeing me the next day. My parents were usually off work the day after Thanksgiving, but my mom sometimes would wander around the malls looking for deals on Black Friday. I wanted to make sure she would be home.

While Thanksgiving seems to be a great celebratory time for most families across America, Mr. Joseph made it clear to me why he didn't have a family dinner as the people around the country did. He was quick to point out the indoctrination of black people in America, whether native or foreign born. While at the dinner table the previous night on Thanksgiving evening, he wanted to make it clear, so that I wouldn't confuse his family dinner with a Thanksgiving celebration. "You see, Kane, we haven't seen Candace in a while, and the best way for any family to celebrate, is over dinner. We wanted to have this dinner tonight to celebrate our daughter and you. I don't want you to think that we subscribe to these white traditions, as most black people in this country do, which promotes white supremacy," he said. I wasn't clear where he was going, so I just listened. "Kane, from the time African people were brought to America, they were forced to celebrate traditions that degrade them and other people. Most black people don't ever question the origin of all the holidays that they celebrate. They all go with the flow, because it's part of the assimilation process into a white dominant culture that forces all people to subscribe to their marginalization of all groups, including Native Americans," he said. "How so?" I asked. "Well, I'm an immigrant in this country, but over time, I made it my business and duty to learn about American history and all the traditions that white people celebrate. It's foolish to stand with the ignorant people who celebrate Thanksgiving every year, but it's the American thing to do. White people have all of us acting like fools. I did it, too, during my first three years in this country. The Haitian people that I was around never took the time to educate themselves, to learn why Thanksgiving was established, and why white people created a holiday to celebrate the slaughter of the Native Americans, people who actually welcomed them with open arms, fed them, provided everything that they needed when they first landed on Plymouth Rock," he said. "That's interesting, because as an African-American, I never learned that history, and never even thought of it that way," I told him. He paused for a minute, as if he were in deep thought, and said to me, "You're not supposed to question anything these white people put in front of you, because they have managed to fool all of us into believing their truth is absolute, even when it's a lie, and all white traditions are good traditions." Mr. Joseph was getting deep with his shit, and I started to question my own humanity as a black American. "Was I supposed to feel guilty for celebrating the annihilation of a group of people?" I questioned in my head. However, Mr. Joseph would bring it all home soon enough. "You see, Kane, white people have been able to go around globe to marginalize and subjugate people of color, murdered them, raped them, stole resources from the indigenous people of Australia, annihilate the indigenous people of the Caribbean, and enslave Africans, because we are all of a different nature from them."

He continued, "Most people of color are very welcoming to outsiders, because they want to learn from them and help them in the most harmonious way, most of the time. However, if you look at the history of white people, they want to control and destroy everything everywhere they go. They also want to explore everything. These bastards want to go to the sun, the moon, the stars, Mars, and wherever they feel they have the right to go. From Africa to

North America, the Caribbean and South America, white people have pretty much annihilated entire races of people everywhere on the planet, just so they can take over and control countries they have no business controlling, and pillage resources that don't belong to them. That is part of their nature, which is why they set out to colonize the entire world. We are not like them," he said. Mr. Joseph sent me into thinking mode, and I had to reflect on all that he said, and I came to the realization that he was right. This government sent my black ass to Iraq to fight in a war that I had no business fighting in. I didn't care about gaining control of Iraqi oil and other resources. We looted Iraq like I had never seen before, and I never once questioned my loyalty to the US government. I was just out there to do a job, and my survival was all that they forced me to think about while training me to murder innocent people. We had no business in Iraq, because we attacked them under the false pretense of violations of weapons of mass destruction that was never proven. I started seeing Mr. Joseph in a whole different light, because he was the type of thinker and philosopher that I needed in my life.

FIRST THING FIRST

The next day, Candace and I woke up very early, so we could make our way to the airport to pick up the rental car, but not before she snuck into the guest room for a quickie with me. I was nervous as hell because her dad and I were getting along so well. The last thing I wanted to do was to disrespect them in their own home, but Candace insisted, and when my baby is horny, I can never resist her. I threw caution to the wind when Candace slid under the covers and wrapped her tongue around her favorite hardened ten-inch, blood-filled delectable sausage. The thrill of being in her parents' house alone was enough to make the experience way more exciting than it actually was, so I was game. With my ears designated to the hallway to listen out for footsteps from her parents, and eyes focused on her luscious lips gliding up and down my hardened member, I wanted all the smoke. I mean, all the freaky shit. My baby never looked so sexy in her natural state, when she snuck into my room with a bonnet on her head, night shirt, and fuzzy flip-flops. "Are you up?" she whispered softly in my ear. As a matter of fact, I had been up for a good hour and wondered if she was up. I didn't have the courage to make my way down the hall to her room, but I sure was glad she came to mine. "I'm up, babe. I've been up, thinking about you and our future together," I told her. She gently kissed my lips, completely ignoring my possible foul morning breath, before making her way down to my chest to lick my nipples softly. I tried to stop her, worried that her parents might hear us, but she insinuated she had no fear. "Stop worrying," she instructed me. "I got this," she reassured me. In my head, the last thing I wanted was for her dad to open the door and find me boning the hell out of his daughter, or worse yet, to find her slobbing on my knob right under his roof. I knew that would be an automatic expulsion from his house with a possible ass whooping. "We're engaged to be married. My parents are not stupid. They know we're fucking," she said. "Yeah, but they don't know we're fucking in their house, and I don't want them to think I'm disrespectful," I told her, sounding like a little bitch. "I'll deal with it," she said assertively, while her mouth took hold of my johnson and held it hostage in the most pleasurable way with the warmth of her mouth and the gliding of her tongue up and down across it. I gave in. I held on to the headboard of the bed to keep it from hitting the wall, while the euphoria of her mouth took over my soul. It's not like I hadn't received fellatio from her before, but this time it was different. The environment added to the excitement of getting caught, and it brought on a different type of danger that stimulated me in a way that I hadn't experienced before. I reached for the back of her head, grabbing her bonnet, to let her know how good she was making me feel. She could sense the intensity as she wrapped her tongue tight around my johnson to give me all the wonderful kingly treatment her mouth could bestow upon me.

My apprehension soon disappeared, as Candace's mouth transported me to a different medium, where no fear existed. I was no longer preoccupied with getting caught by her parents. I was just enjoying the moment. I started to think that my fiancée was a lot freakier than I initially thought, so I had better step up my game. I pulled myself out of Candace's mouth, and pulled her toward the edge of the bed, with her feet dangling over the ground. I spread open her legs to stare at her darkly pink labia. It had been a couple days since I touched her in the most sexual and sensual way, but this was a hurried situation, and I wanted to take her to home plate as quickly as possible. I parted her lips like the red sea with my tongue, then landed it on top of her clitoris to commence the heavenly tongue cleansing she deserved. She never tasted so good. Candace had a habit of being a little loud, so I made sure she grabbed a pillow to cover her mouth, while my tongue explored her erogenous zone. Her legs trembled as my tongue softly swept the tip of her clitoris like a brush made of silk. "Babe, I want you inside me," she whispered, with the understanding that time was not on our side and it could only be a quickie. With my eyes fixated on the door and my ears glued to any possible sound coming from the hallway. I gently pounced on Candace's kitty cat until her discharging secretion validated my efforts. I had a rhythm going with my eyes on the door-knob, my ears stuck to the hallway, and the gyration of my waist while inside her kitty cat. I could sense that she was almost there, so I obliged her because her most intense and pleasurable orgasms were always the result of penile penetration. Candace had a way of letting me know she was about climax by tightening her vaginal muscles and digging her fingers into my chest or back, depending on the position. I wanted her to hurry and get one. I stood still while she grinded on me, but she pulled back. I was looking dead into her greedy eyes and wondered why she didn't just come? Candace was playing a dangerous game, but I was down for anything by then. She moved toward the end of the bed. While holding her legs up on my arms, I slowly slid myself back inside her, and her wetness invaded every inch of me again. This time my rhythm was slower and calculated, because Candace required a particular stroking position to climax quickly. I wanted to control the situation. There was no way I was gonna give her the opportunity to back out from coming this time. I clinched her leg in a way that she couldn't pull away from me. I had learned her ways and became very familiar with her body over time. I stroked her to the left to reach her G-spot. After a few strokes, I could see her body convulsing, and I knew that I also had to go for mine. While Candace was in a trance, I decided to go all in and exploded inside of her. It was one of the best nuts that I had busted in a long while, but it was more exciting because of the allure of getting caught by her parents.

GOODBYE NEW YORK

After my quick session with Candace, I felt like I was walking on pins and needles, as I made my way to the bathroom to take a shower. I hoped that her parents didn't hear her moaning in my room, even though I tried my best to suffocate the sound with a pillow over her mouth. Candace quickly vanished from the room for a quick repose in her own bedroom, as I showered. I brushed my teeth and lathered well under the warm water while thinking about my future with Candace. She was everything that I wanted in a woman; smart, beautiful, sassy, sexy, family oriented, selfless and so much more. The fact that I got along with her family was one less hurdle that I had to worry about. I walked out of the shower feeling clean as a whistle. I was wearing my gym shorts and a t-shirt when I stepped out into the hallway to find Candace standing there, staring at me with wandering eyes and a grin full of love on her face. I couldn't help being head over heels and completely in love with that woman. I smiled at her in a way that assuredly confirmed my devotion and love for her. Candace and I had developed our own love language over time. She knew what I was thinking even before I thought of it. "You better hurry up and take your shower, so we can make our way to the airport," I said to her. She walked toward me while wearing a robe with a towel in her hand and whispered, "I wish I could've showered with you. You look so delicious right now." "Don't tempt me. I don't mind showering twice," I said flirtatiously while brushing up against her, as I quickly walked my ass back to the guestroom.

It didn't take long for Mr. Joseph to knock on my door to check if I was up. He was surprised to find me fully dressed and ready to start my day. His reaction let me know that he wasn't aware of what took place earlier in the room between me and his daughter. I was safe, and still in their good graces. "I'm gonna jump in the shower and get dressed right quick. Would you like to have breakfast before you leave," he asked. I thought about it for a quick second, before I agreed that breakfast would be a good idea. "Sure, Mr. Joseph, breakfast would be great," I told him. I didn't even consult with Candace. I made the decision for her. I didn't do that too often. I figured sitting down for another meal with the family before we left was the best thing, because we weren't going to see them again. We had planned on driving straight to the airport on our way back. "I'll ask my wife to get breakfast ready for everybody," Mr. Joseph assured, before heading to his room.

Mrs. Joseph decided to cook a feast that morning because she knew she wasn't going to see us again that weekend. She made a traditional Haitian breakfast that included scrambled eggs with green peppers, and onions, boiled sweet plantain, turkey bacon and sausage, fresh tomatoes, and more. I was still questioning where that woman found all that strength to always show up as superwoman in the kitchen for her family. Sitting next to my future wife at the breakfast table, and observing the interaction between her parents was enough for me to know that I was embarking on a loving journey, where my children will benefit from the love of their grandparents. Mr. Joseph subtly mentioned to me that he was looking forward to having a grandson one day. I chuckled at the possibility, because I wish to have a son with Candace eventually, too. Her parents made it clear that marriage was teamwork, and they were there for each other through it all. I was about to marry a woman who had a clear understanding of what a marriage is supposed to be like because her parents had given her the best example they possibly could, which was to our benefit.

Time flew by quickly, and before we knew it, eight o'clock had crept up on us. It was time to go. Her dad and I loaded the luggage in his car, and we were off to the airport. On the way to the airport, I got to see a personal side of Mr. Joseph. This man loved his daughter beyond the moon, and he wanted nothing more than the best for her and her complete happiness, which I intended to provide without limitation. He made it clear that he was going to hold me responsible for taking good care of his daughter, and he entrusted me with her care. "Kane, I don't really know you that well, but I trust that I raised my daughter right and well enough, to make the best decision for her life. If she loves you then I have no choice but to love you as a son. So far, you seem like a respectable young man to me, but please understand that I'm willing to do anything and everything in my power to protect and defend my daughter. When it comes to my blood, I don't play. My roots run deep in Haiti, and we embrace our African traditions, ancestry, and heritage, if you know what I mean. And after you marry my daughter and the two of you have children, I will protect them the same way that I would protect my daughter. Please take great care of her, and I wanna take this opportunity to welcome you to the family," Mr. Joseph said out of thin air. I pondered how to respond, but my tongue was tied for a few minutes. I stared into space, my mind wandering and trying to think of an appropriate response to Mr. Joseph. "Thank you, sir. I respect everything that you just said. I'm not here to waste your daughter's time. I think I fell in love with her the very first time I laid eyes on her. I have never met a woman like your daughter. She's very special, and I'm sure you have a lot to do with that. I plan on honoring your daughter in every way possible, and I want her to make you and your wife proud of the decision she made by choosing me as a partner and future husband. I'm impressed with your family setting, and I hope to one day provide a great structure for the family that I plan on having with your daughter. Just like you, I would put my life on the line to protect and defend your daughter, and our future children, sir. Thanks again for welcoming me into your family. I'm happy to be part of your family." Mr. Joseph quickly turned his eyes from the road to look at me and said, "My man," as he reached out to dap me. I could see Candace smirking out of the corner of my eyes, at her dad's attempt to sound cool. She also knew that her dad and I had connected, and was very happy about that. I had passed the test.

We soon arrived at the car rental destination. After making sure we were able to secure a car, Mr. Joseph departed, but not before he gave Candace a long hug, and shook my hand in a proud and comforting way. "I'll see you guys soon. Candace knows how nosey and protective her mother can be, so we'll more than likely come to Atlanta to visit you guys soon. She's gonna want to know how her daughter's living and where. She's way more protective than me. I'm the easy one, but she likes you as well," Mr. Joseph said. "You sure it's just mommy who's nosey? I'm sure you want to know how I'm living, too, Daddy. Thanks for the ride, Daddy. I'll call you when we get to Boston. Love you," Candace told her dad. "Thank you, Mr. Joseph. I'll see you again soon," I said as I bid adieu to him.

BEANTOWN,
HERE WE COME

After picking up a 2020 Toyota, Highlander SUV from the rental car's parking lot, I quickly went to Google Maps on my phone to find directions from New York to my parents' house in Dorchester, a section of Boston. Honestly, I only needed directions to navigate my way from LaGuardia airport to Interstate 95. From there, it was easy to find my way home without any problems. I had driven to New York with a couple of my boys for weekend hangouts on more than a few occasions. I knew my way around a little. For almost a good hour until we reached the last toll out of New York, I listened to the directions on the phone while Candace held my hand, and stayed alert to make sure we didn't miss any turns. We worked as a team to navigate our way out of the city. Once we reached Interstate 95 North, she moved herself closer to me, uploaded her favorite music mix from her phone into the Bluetooth in the car, and cozied up to me. While I kept my eyes on the road and left hand on the wheel, my right hand sensually caressed Candace's arms and legs, making my presence felt. "You know sometimes your touch alone makes me feel safe, protected, and loved by you," she uttered. I felt a little tingle inside when she revealed that. "I feel the same way about you, babe. I know you have my back, and always will. I'm not afraid to love you and pour my all into you and this relationship. I don't want to ever be without you. There's no place else for me. You are it for me. I love you with all my heart," I told her. She smiled and said, "How am I supposed to compete with all that sweetness and greatness? I'm not going anywhere either, babe. You're more of a man than I have ever dreamed that I could've found. I want to love you for the rest of my life. I want to have your babies, be your friend, your lover, the whore that you fantasize about, your wife, and everything that you need me to be to keep you happy. I love you with all my being and soul." It was pretty comforting to know that Candace was dedicated to me as much as I was to her. I was always confident that we had a strong relationship, but confirmation with words is always comforting. I wanted to give this woman my best.

We drove in silence for about a half hour, while listening to our favorite jams... well, Candace's favorite jams. Candace and I communicated simply through touch. She was the most affectionate woman that I had ever been with, and she brought out my own affectionate side toward her. The intent wasn't always sexual, but there were times when Candace and I couldn't resist each other. I kept my eyes on the road and my mind on our future. I imagined all types of ways that I was going to make her happy, and how she would reciprocate the love and happiness that I planned on bringing to her. I even imagined how our children would look while looking lost in the distance, and then she woke me out of my stupor by asking, "What do you think of my parents?" The question wasn't as awkward as it was unexpected. I was just fantasizing about a perfect life with her, and then she hit me with that question. Of course, I admired the relationship her parents share, and I thought I made it obvious that I was fond of them. "What do you mean by what do I think of your parents?" I retorted. "Do you like them? You think you'll be able to get along with them and blend as a family? I know my mom can be difficult, but she's only acting the way she is, because she just met you. I know that she likes you, otherwise, she wouldn't have gotten up to make us breakfast this morning." Candace was going a mile a minute before I got a chance to answer her question. "Babe, your mom is wonderful. I have a mother as well, and I don't anticipate that everything will be perfect between you guys when you first meet. Parents have to adjust to their children's spouses, just as the spouses sometimes have to adjust to them. At the end of the day, it's about us," I told her. She stared at me for the longest time before uttering, "Babe, I don't want you to get this confused. When you marry me, you're marrying my family. My parents are gonna want to be involved in the lives of our children, and they're gonna want to keep them during summer vacations and any other time we are willing to send them to New York to spend time with them. It's part of my Haitian customs and culture, so it's not just about us. I want to be clear on that," she said. I quickly responded, "Well, I don't see anything wrong with that, but our relationship must always come first. We can't allow outside forces and people to influence our relationship. We have to be dedicated to one another, and we must always fight on behalf of one another no matter what. I'm always going to take your side and support you in every way. My parents will never come before you. I hope you understand what I'm saying." My statement was firm. She shook her head in agreement with me, but I wasn't convinced that we were on the same page. "I get it, babe. I'm not going to allow our cultural differences to create a wedge between us or my family. I'm just warning you that my parents might become a little overbearing after we have children. We're not gonna be able to go years without giving them access to their grandchildren. I still want to know your opinion of them, though," she said. I don't know, maybe I wasn't obvious enough with her dad. "Babe, I think your parents are great, but I especially like your dad, because I connected with him. Your mom is a work in progress, but she's a great woman. She did a wonderful job raising you. I'm sure I'm gonna grow to love her like a second mom. I have nothing negative to say about your family. They're great people," I told her. "Well, babe, I'm glad you like them, because I can tell that they like you, too. I hope that your parents are proud that you chose me. I'm looking forward to getting to know them. I just want us to be one big happy family," she said. "Don't worry, babe, they're gonna love you," I assured her.

Time flew by as we were conversing about how our perception of our parents. Before I knew it, a couple of hours had gone by, and we were in Rhode Island. I didn't even realize we had gotten to Rhode Island so quickly. My experiences driving through Rhode Island had never been great, so I carefully set my cruise control to 55-65 miles per hour, in case one of these racist state troopers in Rhode Island decided to take their bad day out on me. No sooner did I set my cruise control, I saw the blue lights, as an officer pulled up behind from a speed trap under a bridge. I was confident that I was not speeding. There were plenty of cars passing me on the left, as I was in the slower lane on the right. I could tell he was gunning for me because he moved all the way to the right to pull up behind me. "I'm getting pulled over, babe," I told Candace. "For what!? You're not speeding. Stay calm, babe. Hopefully, he's not an asshole," she said, trying to comfort me. She was the one who was heated, because I was getting pulled over for absolutely no reason. I can see the trooper putting on his hat, as he approached my car, trying his best to look intimidating. I slowly put down my window with both hands on the wheel. "License and registration please," the trooper said to me. "I'm reaching for my license in my back pocket, sir. My registration is in the glove compartment, and my fiancée is going to grab it," I told him. I didn't want to give this white dude any reason to show aggression toward me or Candace, especially during the climate of Trumpism across the country. I grabbed the registration from Candace and handed it along with my driver's license to the officer. "Do you know why I pulled you over?" he asked. "No sir," I answered. "The speed limit is 65 and you're barely doing 55. Are you hiding something? I see you're coming from New York," he said, as if the New York license plates on the car weren't obvious enough. "Sir, did you seriously pull me over for driving slower than the speed limit posted, while I'm in the slow lane? Is that even legal?" I asked. I could see Candace getting pissed off out of the corner of my eyes, but I squeezed her hand to keep her calm. Last thing I needed was for Candace to get me riled up, or allowed her to get riled up because a racist piece of shit decided to pull me over. "I decide what's legal and illegal. I'm the law here," he arrogantly boasted. "I don't know about you being the law, but you work to enforce the law, and I have not broken any law," I said to him. Candace kept her camera in a position to record my interaction with the officer, after logging on to her account on Instagram to go live. Once he looked over and noticed that Candace was recording him, he started changing his tune. "Well, stopping you was more of a welfare check. Sometimes people drive slow because of mechanical issues with their car," he lied. "Thanks for your concern, but the car is perfectly fine. I'll take back my license and registration," I boldly told him. I'm not sure if he wanted the business or not that day, but he quickly handed me my license and registration and told us to have a nice day. I was ready to give him the business because I knew he had no reason to pull me over.

Though I had avoided a confrontation with the cop, there was still a couple of hours before I reached home, and there was the possibility that I could get pulled over again by another asshole cop in Rhode Island, or an even greater racist asshole state police officer, once I reached Massachusetts. The goal was to make it to my parents' house safely in one piece. I couldn't believe it's the twenty-first century and I still have to worry about Driving While Black. These white supremacist agents are all over, and black people can't seem to get away from them. Candace and I listened to our music, while I followed every possible traffic rule until we got to Boston. Needless to say, I didn't feel safe until after I walked into my parents' house.

MEETING HIS PARENTS

When we arrived in Boston, I didn't know what to expect at first. After getting off an exit that said, "Milton," from the interstate, Kane drove through a nice quiet suburban town that he described to me as Milton. It was a nice upper middle class community, but he cautioned that the cops in that area were racist, too. He drove down State Route 28 until we reached a street that he called Dorchester Avenue, near his parents' house in Dorchester, where he grew up. There was a sharp contrast between Dorchester and Milton, even though the two towns bordered one another. The hood in Boston was a little different than the hoods that I was used to in Brooklyn. He drove down Dorchester Avenue until he made a few turns to reach his final destination on Evans Street. We pulled up to a nice two-family house not too far from a park. The house looked like it was recently renovated with new siding and well-kept, overall. "I thought you said you grew up in the hood?" I joked with him. "This is the hood. Don't let the quietness and the houses fool you," he said. "Well, I'll take this hood any day over Brownsville, Brooklyn. It seems like a quiet enough neighborhood to me," I told him. While Kane and I were talking, a dude walked up, filled with glee, and said, "Yo Kane, you're back?" Kane turned around to see a childhood friend he hadn't seen since he left Boston. "Yo, Jamal, what's going on? How you been, bruh?" Kane asked with enthusiasm and happiness in his voice. "Man, you know? We're out here trying to survive in these rough streets. You know a couple of them guys are gone, and what-cha-ma-call-it is locked up," he said. "Word? Damn, bruh. That's sad to hear. I'm just getting here, but I'll get up wit ya," Kane said in his hood vernacular. I liked that he could navigate the hood and the corporate world. "How long you in town for?" Jamal asked. "Just for a couple of days, but stop by the crib tomorrow or something so we can kick it for a few, ok? I'll be here," Kane told him. "Aight, fam, I'll do that. It's nice seeing you," he told Kane as they exchanged a manly hug before he departed.

As I took inventory of Kane's neighborhood, I saw nothing dangerous or threatening about where he grew up, at least the section where he lived didn't look dangerous to me. After gentrification, I remember that Bedstuy no longer looks like a place where crackheads used to roam the streets at all hours of the night, and break into people's cars to steal their jack. His neighborhood could've well been gentrified, but that was just an assumption on my part. As we unloaded the car to walk up the stairs, a middle-aged woman of average height and weight, stood at the top of the steps to welcome Kane into her arms. I caught the resemblance right away. Kane looks just like his mom. Like a little boy who hadn't seen his mom in a long time, Kane dropped the bags on the ground to rush up the steps to give his mother a big hug and lifted her off the ground. "My boy is finally home. My baby, how I missed you?" his mother said as she sighed loudly. "I miss you, too, Mom," Kane responded as if she was a comfortable, warm blanket wrapped around his body. I had never seen that vulnerable side of him. I never pegged him to be a mama's boy, but the boy loves his mama. I stood there admiring their embrace, and low-keyed hope to be loved by her just as much one day, as a daughter-in-law. "So, who do we have here?" his mother asked as she gazed my way. "I'm sorry. Mom, this is Candace, and Candace, this is my mom," Kane formally introduced us. I walked up the steps to meet her and gave her a hug. "You must be the young lady who's been keeping my son's mind busy in Atlanta. All he does is talk about you, but he didn't tell me he was bringing you home to meet the family," she said. "I hope that's not a problem, ma'am," I said to her. "Oh no, it's never a problem for family to stop by. My son wouldn't just bring anybody home, so he must think you're very special and must be very sure about you," Mrs. Black said. It was comforting to know that he wouldn't just bring anybody home to meet his parents. His mom seemed like a nice and warm woman, but I could tell she was a little overprotective of

Kane. That was normal, as far as I was concerned.

After making our way inside the house, Kane walked toward the living room and found his dad sitting on the couch, He quickly rushed to hug him. "What up, pops? You look like you're eating good. What mom's been feeding you?" Kane asked jokingly. I could tell right away he had a special relationship with his dad. "How've you been, son? You're looking just as good as your daddy. You better thank me for them good genes," his father joked. "I know y'all ain't acting like I didn't have anything to do with his handsomeness," his mother chimed in. "Aight, maybe he got your eyebrows, but everything else is from me," his dad joked again, as he lifted Kane up in a tight hug. "Who's this beautiful young flower with ya?" his dad asked. Kane looked toward me, smiled and said, "This is my fiancée, Candace. I'm engaged y'all." His mom suddenly moved toward me to grab my left hand. "Engaged? Let me see that ring," she said as she held my hand up, shaking her head with approval for the ring. "Yes, mom. Yes, dad, Candace and I got engaged. You're gonna have a daughter-in-law," he told them. "Any fiancée of my son's is welcomed into my house, especially when she's as beautiful as you. Kane knows if you were butt ugly, I would've kicked you out right away," his dad joked, before turning to Kane to say, with a serious look on his face, "How did you manage to land such a beautiful young lady?" I was a little shy, but not nervous. "She is beautiful," his mom reaffirmed. "Thank you," I responded. "She's great. You guys are gonna love her," Kane told them. I had never been the center of attention like that, so it felt a little awkward that I was being discussed by everyone present. Kane noticed my discomfort and quickly changed the subject. "I think we're a little tired from waking up so early this morning to hit the road. We're gonna go to the room for a little nap," he said to his parents. I didn't know if the sleeping arrangements were going to be the same as we had at my parents' house, so I waited to be walked to the guestroom. "I'm sure you know your brother, Jeff, has his own place now, so we use his room as a guestroom. You and Candace can stay in his room," Mr. Black said. I was surprised that his parents were allowing us to stay in the same room. Kane picked up the luggage and asked me to follow him. We walked into a bedroom that looked like it had been decorated by his mom to make her guests feel comfortable and at home. There was a queen bed with a stained wooden headboard, a nightstand on the right side of the bed, a dresser on the left side, and, an armoire across from the bed, with a television inside of it. The room looked cozy and clean. I'm a woman, so I tend to pay more attention to the small details. I was happy that I was gonna get to sleep with Kane for the two days that I was there.

Before we got to napping, Kane stepped out of the room, while I stood beside him, and said to his mother, "Mom, can you wake us up around 6 pm, so we can go out to dinner?" Kane asked his mom. "Out to dinner? My son just came to see me after all this time, and you think you're gonna take us out to dinner? You need a taste of your mother's home-cooked meal. We can do this dinner date thing another time. I've got to feed my baby. We have plenty of food in the fridge left over from Thanksgiving dinner. I cooked all your favorites," his mother said. "So, you're gonna offer him all of my favorite foods that I was looking forward to eating tonight just cause he came home?" his dad joked. His mom jokingly cut her eyes at his dad and said, "You know we've got more than enough food in the fridge for everyone to eat. Candace, you don't mind eating leftovers, right? Food always tastes better the next day, anyway." "Leftovers are fine, I responded. I was just happy to meet his family. I didn't care what we ate. His father smiled at his mother and said with laughter, "Your mother put her foot in that food yesterday, it was so good. I might have to fight you for seconds. Her cooking is the reason why I have this big ass stomach right now. She's feeding me too good." Kane looked at the two of them and shook his head. "I know some people don't like to eat leftovers, so you don't have to eat it if you don't want to," her mother said to me. "I don't mind. You're right, leftovers always taste better the next day. I would rather eat your cooking on my first day here, anyway," I told her. "Good. I'll have the food ready and all warmed up by the time you guys wake up," she said. "That's if I don't eat it all before y'all wake up," his father joked. "Don't pay my daddy no mind, he thinks he's Steve Harvey, always coming with the jokes," Kane said. Actually, I thought his dad was hilarious and a breath of fresh air from what I was used to with my father. I enjoyed it. "Go ahead, y'all go on and take that nap. We'll see y'all later for dinner," his mom said.

It didn't long for Kane and I to fall into a deep sleep after shutting our eyes. A few hours later, we woke up to the house smelling like well-spiced greens, macaroni and cheese, baked turkey, mashed potatoes, white rice and red beans, and cornbread warming up over the stove and the oven. By then his younger sister, Cynthia, had also come home, and I got to meet her. She was a freshman in college and was home for the Thanksgiving break. After Kane and I brushed our teeth, we met everyone in the dining room for dinner. As we were about to sit down for dinner, the doorbell rang. It was Jeff, Kane's younger brother. Mrs. Black had told him Kane was in town, so he immediately rushed over to partake in the festivities. Jeff was a younger version of Kane, but he favored his mother a little more, as far as his looks. He was also taller than Kane, but a little burly like his father. After the formal introductions, everyone sat at the table to eat the leftovers from Thanksgiving dinner. I'm not even gonna lie, I don't know what the food tasted like when it was freshly cooked, but that shit was the bomb the next day. I could tell Kane enjoyed his mother's cooking because he couldn't stop licking his fingers. His siblings also had no problem eating the same food twice in two days, and I understood why. Mrs. Black was a great cook, and I enjoyed every single dish she made.

After dinner, it was time to get to know the family, and for the family to get to know me. As black traditions go, we found ourselves playing a game of spades at the table while casually conversing. "So, Candace, where are your folks from?" Mr. Black asked. I was trying to read the room, in order to gauge the reaction that I might get after revealing my family background. "My parents are from Haiti, but I was born in Brooklyn," I revealed. His sister jumped into the conversation right away, before anyone else could say anything. It was almost as if she was trying to take the opportunity to take the focus off me, because she knew something I didn't know. It could've also very well been that she wanted to tell her own parents to set aside their prejudice because black people are not homogeneous, and we can find love in each other. I didn't know, but my mind was wandering. "The guy I'm dating now, his parents are from Jamaica," she said, with a big smile on her face. "I didn't know you were dating one of them immigrants," Mrs. Black said, with emphasis on immigrants, with much ignorance. I could sense the discomfort on Kane's face right away, and he saw my own discomfort when he glanced over at me. However, before he could jump up to defend me, his feisty little sister had more to say. "Ma, stop with the ignorance. There are tons of good immigrant people out there. You can't judge people based on what the media tells you about them. They do the same thing to African-Americans every day. I don't know what you mean by one of them immigrants, but I love my Jamaican boo," she proclaimed. Before things got too serious, Mr. Black intervened and said, "I'm sure your mother didn't mean any harm. You know how your mother can be sometimes. Candace, please continue to tell us about your family. What do your parents do for a living?" The temperature in the room had gone from warm to cold, and I didn't feel that Kane's mom's statement was welcoming to me. However, before I could answer his dad, Kane stood up and said, "Mom, I know you've had your issues with some of the immigrant folks in Boston, but I'm gonna need you to set aside your prejudice, because my fiancée's background is Haitian, and there's nothing you can do to change that. In addition, I've met her parents and spent a couple of days at their house, and they welcomed me like a son. They are good decent people, and I'm gonna need you to understand that my fiancée, Candace, came from a great family, and she's good people as well. As a matter of fact, she's a great person, which is why I chose her, and I'm gonna need you to accept her and respect my choice." Kane nipped it in the bud right away. I looked over to see a look of pride on his father's face, for having stood for me. However, I couldn't make out the look on Mrs. Black's face. It was just a blank stare into nowhere. She probably felt attacked, but I didn't know the history between her and her children. "Mom, times are changing. Black people come in all shapes and sizes, and they are from every corner of the earth. We can't allow our differences to create more division among us. African-Americans are not the only group of black people who have contributed to the development of this country. The black Diaspora is a collective effort. Malcolm X's mother was from Grenada, the great Marcus Garvey was from Jamaica, Jean Baptist Point Du Sable who discovered Chicago was from Haiti, Minister Louis Farrakhan's family is from Trinidad, and the list of great black people from immigrant families who have contributed to this country is endless. We know it's difficult to accept change, but you can't help who your children choose to love, and you definitely shouldn't allow your prejudice against another black person to get in the way of getting to know them, because one of your children loves them. I know y'all don't want me to start dating white boys, right? At least I'm keeping it black. I'm in love with my Jamaican boyfriend, and I support Kane's choice," his sister said. I think it was time to try to get past that conversation, because nobody was interested in finishing the game of spades anymore. Just like that, we went from jovial to serious.

From the time Jeff walked through the door, I could tell his demeanor was timid and quiet. He wasn't a jokester like his dad, a smooth operator like Kane, or feisty like his sister. He lived in his own world. Still, he wanted to take the opportunity to join the conversation to let his parents know that he was dating a woman from Trinidad. "While we're on the subject of dating, does it make a difference that my girlfriend is from Trinidad?" he asked. His mother looked over at him and said, "You too? They got my baby, too?" I don't think she realized the favoritism she displayed in that moment, but it was obvious that Jeff was her favorite child. I'm not sure she expected all three of her children to be dating the Black United Nations, but that's what was going on. Reason would prevail when Mr. Black said, "As long as the kids are happy with their choices. That's the only thing that should matter. We're gonna have black babies, no matter who they end up marrying. Personally, I have no problem with you, Candace. I also know that my wife has no problem with you as well. She has the right to express herself, but we'll work on her opinion." All the kids shook their heads in unison. Mrs. Black was alone in her prejudice. "Mom, would you not have dated Dad if he was from another country? Do you think he would've been a different person just because he might've been born somewhere else? Jeff reasoned. "Mom, just think about the life you would've missed out on, if you had decided not to date dad, because he was from a different place?" Kane asked. I felt like everyone was piling on her, so I offered my own olive branch. "Mrs. Black, if it's any consolation, I understand where you're coming from, because as the daughter of immigrant parents, I grew up listening to my mom talking about her own prejudice toward African-Americans. I also worried about the way she would react to Kane when I brought him home. Still, that was a chance that I was willing to take because I love Kane, and I want to be with Kane. I'm sure Kane probably felt the exact same way when he thought about bringing me here to meet his parents. The gap between black immigrants and African-Americans is something that my generation will probably have to bridge, but I can only worry about Kane for now.

I know that I love him, and nothing that you say can force me out of his life. No disrespect," I expressed. It sounded as if I was giving a speech, while standing on top of a podium, but Kane and his siblings started clapping out of the blue, and even Mr. Black was smiling. I wasn't sure if I made the right choice by voicing my opinion, but Mrs. Black stood up, stared at me, and said, "I respect that. Any woman who's willing to take the risk to stand up in a respectful manner, to the mother of her fiancée is worth adding to the family. I'm sorry for my rude comment about immigrants. I'm sure we're gonna learn a lot about each other, as this relationship flourishes." Those were probably the most comforting words that I could've heard. "There you go, mom. We knew you had the potential to be open-minded," Cynthia said while smiling at her mom. Everybody moved in for a group hug to smooth things over. From that day, I never had to worry about how Mrs. Black felt about me. She was sincere, apologetic, and just wanted her son to be happy at the end of the day, just like most parents.

The weekend went by without a hitch. I got to learn so much about Kane's family, while they discovered many things about me, my family, and the struggles and history of Haitian people in the world, ever since they dared stand up to debunk white superiority, supremacy, and imperialism. In the midst of talking all that Haiti had to overcome, in order to be acknowledged by America and the rest of the imperialist nations as a sovereign republic, Mr.

Black started recollecting a racist incident of his own, that he experienced as a teenager walking home from Ashmont station in the early 1980's. After listening to a couple of my historical facts about Haiti, Mr. Black almost welled up, as he recollected his near-death experience at the hands of racist and cowardly white men who attacked him for no reason. "I'm gonna tell you all a story that I have never told to anyone before," Mr. Black started. "Back in the early 80'ss, I used to go downtown Boston to meet my friends, so we could hang out. We were all from different parts of the city, but downtown was the place where we used to hang out on Saturdays. I would hop on the train to meet with them, and I'd catch the train back to go home. One day after leaving my friends, I took the train to Ashmont station as usual, and I started making my way up Fuller Street to go home. As I walked half a block up the street, I heard somebody call me a nigger. I turned around to see an older white man walking toward me, but I didn't back down. I ran toward him to smack the word out of his mouth, and he took off running. I was probably 15 years old at the time. After he took off, I turned around to continue my walk home. Before I could make it to the top of the hill on the black side of the street, a pick-up truck pulled up with about 10 white boys with baseball bats, and they beat the shit outta me. I was covered in blood, and someone drove me to Carney Hospital. I was in a hospital for a few days before I recovered from my injuries. I was beaten to a pulp, but no bones were broken. My parents wanted to report it to the police, but I already knew the police weren't gonna do shit. I told them not to bother because I had my own plans. Though I was not in a gang, but the guys who called themselves a gang in my neighborhood were all cool with me. They had heard about what happened to me, and they were ready for revenge after I got out the hospital. As soon as I healed enough to walk, I went behind the Thompson Middle School to find the "gang" to see how we were going to handle my situation. T-Money was the leader of the crew, and he had an appetite for violence, especially against the white boys by Ashmont station, because he had been jumped by them as well in the past. We decided we were gonna put an end to their jumping black people, once and for all." Mr. Black had all of our attention. "How come you never mentioned this story to me before?" Mrs. Black asked. "You've always seen me as this big guy who can protect you. I couldn't tell you a story about a time when I felt helpless." She looked at him, and raised his chin, and said, "Babe, you were not helpless. You were young, by yourself, and a group of men jumped you. I know you can defend yourself." The story was captivating enough that everyone was anxiously waiting to hear the conclusion to the story. "What happened next, Dad?" Cynthia asked.

"Oh yes, after T-Money decided we would take revenge, we came up with a plan to hotwire four cars, got some bats, wore ski masks, and took a trip down to Dorchester Ave., where the white boys were known to hang out. All four stolen cars were loaded with about 5 people in each car, so we were 20 deep. We pulled up by the station, and as luck would have it, the guys who jumped me were standing against the wall drinking beer openly. Back then, no one had cell phones. People had to use a payphone to call 911. We dropped 2 guys by the payphones, designated to guard them, so nobody could call the police, and we jumped out the car and beat the living crap out of every single white boy who was out there drinking. We caught them off-guard, so they didn't have any weapons with them. We used the bats to put a beating of a lifetime on these white boys, the same way they did to me. By the time the police were called, we were long gone. All the cars were stolen, so there was no way they were going to find any of us. To this day, I still get satisfaction from that vengeful day," Mr. Black said with a grin on his face. "Pops got gangster on them," Kane said. Cynthia crossed over to high-five her dad. Jeff went around dapping everybody as if he took part in the fight. Kane wished he could've been there to apply his own punishment on the white boys. The entire family rejoiced that Mr. Black was able to avenge a malicious beating.

I was happy to learn that Mr. Black and his family weren't the "turning the other cheek" type of people. They were fighters. I love that about them. I came from a family of fighters. My bloodline is revolutionary, and I intend to fight whenever I'm faced with adversities. "So, Candace, you didn't finish telling us what it is that your parents do for work," Mr. Black said to me. The room was back to a jovial atmosphere. "My mother's nurse and my dad is an engineer," I told him. "That's good. You came from a hard-working family. You two will do well together, you and my son," Mr. Black said proudly. I shook my head to agree. Everything was all good again. I tried as much as possible to answer every question they asked about Haitian culture, because there were many stereotypes they had heard about Haiti and Haitian people. Kane even demonstrated his own knowledge about Haiti to his family whenever they asked a question that he knew the answer to.

Our journey as a couple had begun, and Kane and I were on a smooth path to marital bliss. I spent the rest of the weekend visiting local black-owned businesses on Saturday with Mrs. Black and Cynthia. We also got a chance to go to brunch, a spa, and the nail salon, while Kane hung out with his dad and brother. Overall, it was a great experience, and I looked forward to extending our blended families. There were no more quarrels or disagreements for the rest of the weekend. Kane was happy to see that his family had taken a liking to me after learning more about me. I'm not saying his mom was converted completely as a fan of mine, but she was very cordial and open to learning. I could understand that she might've been disappointed that her children weren't bringing home the types of people they had hoped for them to date or marry, but that's the part of life where most people have to learn to make adjustments. I'm almost certain my parents would've preferred for me to marry a man of Haitian decent but that's not where my heart is. My heart is with Kane, and it'll forever belong to Kane. We all know that time flies when we're having fun, but Sunday came so quickly, it felt like a blizzard.

Kane and I woke up very early on Sunday morning for the long drive back to New York to catch our flight back to Atlanta. His mother insisted on making us breakfast before we left, because she knew there was a possibility she may not see us again until the wedding. We couldn't deny her the opportunity to spend another special moment with her son, so we agreed to breakfast. She made the best scrambled eggs, grits, and fried fish. We talked more about our future plans to establish ourselves first, before having children, with his parents, and how we wanted them to be involved in their lives. Mrs. Black couldn't wait to become a grandmother. Kane asked her not to rush the process, because we had a lot more to accomplish before we became parents. Finally, after breakfast, we had to say our goodbyes. A hug fest with everyone took place for about 10 minutes in the kitchen, before we grabbed our bags to head to the car. As we were making our way out, Cynthia ran toward the front door to catch us. "Y'all are leaving without saying goodbye?" she asked with curiosity. "Cynt, you were sleeping. I didn't wanna wake you up. You know you're my favorite sis. I was letting you catch up on your beauty sleep," Kane told her. She smiled and said, "I'm your only sis, and I better be your favorite. Thanks for making a great choice in choosing a sister-in-law for me," she said jokingly after hugging her brother. "I thought I was choosing a great wife for me?" he retorted jokingly, while Cynthia made her way toward me for a hug. "Please take good care of my brother. He's a good man. I hope he told you about the many times that I ran away from the crazy house, so you better treat him good or you'll see me. I love you, though," she said after her little casual comical threat. "I'm gonna take great care of him. He deserves the best care from his partner, and I will always be there for him. Love you, too. See you guys again soon," I said, before finally hopping in the car to leave, so we wouldn't miss our flight.

CANDACE AND I

Considering things could've gone a lot worse, Candace and I were lucky to have great understanding parents who blessed our union and welcomed us as part of their families. My mom is not always the easiest person to get to know, but she loves her family, and will always put the family's needs first, even ahead of her own needs. I'm glad she realized she was being unfair to Candace and offered a heartfelt apology for it. I can't even describe the ways I love this woman. My mother has always been there for me, and it is those same qualities that my mom possesses that I find attractive in Candace. I'd hoped for a less eventful interaction with the cops on the drive back to New York from Boston. No sooner did we hit Interstate 95 South when Candace comfortably reached for my hand, and leaned her head on my right shoulder, as she always does when I'm driving long distance, to remind me that she's always with me. It was a nice breezy but sunny day, and traffic was moving right along. We had about six hours before our flight departed. I wanted to take my time and kept my speed just a little above the posted limit to avoid getting a speeding ticket. This time,

I didn't want to get pulled over for driving under the speed limit. The ride was going smooth, and out of the blue Candace said to me, "This is something you really want, right? We're not getting married because you feel you owe it to me, right?" I didn't see that coming, nor did I know how to reply to it. I was caught off guard. "What did you just say?" I asked her with this obscure look on my face. "I just want to make sure we're getting married because this is what both of us want. I don't want to marry someone who feels it's a duty to marry me, because we've been dating for a while," she said to me. I was trying to figure out where the conversation was headed, but to remove all doubts, I grabbed her face, turn it to me, planted a big wet kiss on her lips, and told her, "Woman, I love you, and I plan on loving you for the rest of my life. Don't ever doubt my love for you. My life has been wonderful since we've met, and I know that I don't want to live the rest of my life without you." I don't know if she was looking for confirmation, or what brought that on, but I assured her my decision to marry her was based on, not just my love for her, but all the positive changes she had brought into my life, and the great things that I envision she was going to bring to our future.

After pondering for a minute, I realized why Candace wanted to make sure I was marrying her because I love her, and not for some other foolish reason. I remember her telling me the extreme circumstances her parents faced when they first moved to America, and how they leaned on one another to make it. "Babe, I know you're not referencing your parents' situation when they met, to analyze why we're getting married, right?" I asked her. She immediately sat up in her seat, so she could look me straight in my eyes before speaking. "It's not just about my parents getting married because they needed each other to make it here in America, it's about your own story that you told me about your own parents and why they got married. I'm not saying that we should have a fairy tale relationship, but I want our love to be on totally solid ground, where we don't have to find reasons outside of our love, in order to get married. I feel that a lot of black folks get married out of necessity. Either someone gets pregnant, and they marry to avoid having a child out of wedlock, or they marry because of financial necessities in order to survive. I don't want that for us. I want us to have a natural loving relationship," she told me. I guess her point of view was fair. There was no ulterior reason for me to marry her other than love. I wanted to assure her that I was making the right decision to love her for who she is, and forever. "Babe, I understand where you're coming from, but I believe that you should be 100% certain of my love for you by now. I love you with every fiber of my being, babe. There's no going back, and I'm never going to regret my decision to marry you. I hope you feel the same way," I told her. She looked straight into my eyes, and said, "I know, babe. I just want to make sure we are on the same page, that you know I will love you forever, and I will put you and my family first, always. I don't want us to be like other couples who wish they never got married. I want us to fight for this relationship forever," she revealed. "It will be forever. No need to worry. I love you," I said while pursing up my lips to kiss her. She pursed up her own lips to kiss me, and said, "I love you, too, babe."

We didn't say much during the rest of the ride, but Candace made her physical presence felt by touching my thighs, rubbing my shoulders, and planting kisses on me sporadically all the way to New York. It was the most joyous long-distance driving I had ever done. My mind was finally at peace, because I no longer had to worry about my family accepting Candace. My brother, sister, father, and mother were all on board. It was just a matter of discussing and planning the wedding with Candace. I didn't know if she wanted a big or a small wedding. I also didn't know where the wedding was going to take place, because we lived in Atlanta, while our families lived in New York and Boston. As far as I knew, everything was cool between us to get married, but our parents hadn't met yet. We had a few months before the wedding was to take place, and we wanted to make sure we got the meet and greet among the parents scheduled and out of the way. What better time to do it than sooner, right?

Candace and I arrived at the airport just in time to catch our flight after dropping off the rental car. While on the plane, we started discussing the type of wedding we wanted, and we both agreed on a destination wedding, which gave us the opportunity to kill two birds with one stone. We didn't have to pay extra for a honeymoon. Since Candace and I had never been to Haiti together, and when she went to Haiti with her parents, she stayed with family. We wanted to go to a nice resort in Haiti to get married. Since we got engaged in the fall, we wanted a summer wedding, so we set the date for July 26th, 2008. We wanted to give ourselves and the people we love, enough time to save their money to fly to Haiti to join us in celebrating our union. Candace chose Haiti because she wanted me to become familiar with the place that birthed her parents, and also the fact that her grandparents were still living there, would make it easier for them to attend the wedding as well. While on the plane, we threw around ideas about budget, the type of dress she wanted to wear, as well as the reception. We both agreed it didn't make sense to spend more than fifteen thousand dollars on our wedding. We didn't want to start our lives in debt. The budget was doable, and we'd still have a little money left in our savings. In addition, we didn't have to worry about paying for a honeymoon, because we'd planned on extending our stay at the hotel after the wedding. Candace figured we would take the opportunity to explore Haiti during our honeymoon. She, herself hadn't explored Haiti much. Her familiarity with the country was limited to the places where her grandparents lived in St. Marc and the capital city of Port-Au-Prince. I was actually excited and looking forward to learning more about Haitian culture. However, before we could plan our wedding, we had to make sure that our parents met. We agreed it would be best if our parents came to Atlanta for a weekend, and we could plan different activities for them. There was no better time for family than the Christmas holidays. Though Candace's family didn't necessarily celebrate Christmas, they were open to coming to Atlanta to meet my parents. My mom and dad were more than thrilled to finally take a mini vacation away from Boston. Everything was set. Candace and I created an itinerary for them that included visits to the King Center, the High Museum of Art, the Georgia Aquarium, Centennial Park, and a few restaurants.

WHEN THE
IN-LAWS MEET

I never anticipated any problems between my parents and Candace's parents, because they were cool and laid back people who wanted the best for their daughter. However, my mom surprised me when she started asking so many invasive questions. To a certain degree, Trump didn't only influence the minds of racists, he also influenced the minds of some black people. After their formal introduction, my mother rudely asked the Josephs how long they had been in this country, and if they were here legally. It wasn't so much the question, but when and how my mother asked the question, so abruptly after meeting the family. Even my dad was taken by surprise. "How long have you guys been in America, and did you come here legally on a plane?" my mom ignorantly asked. I had no idea how Candace's dad had to traverse the roughest seas in the Caribbean to make it here, but he took the question personally and wanted to leave right after he met my parents. Even Candace was a little disturbed by my mother's forward question. As a matter of fact, everyone at the dinner table was taken aback by her derogatory mindset, as it related to immigrants. It was as if Trump himself had descended from the sky and into the restaurant to join our conversation and dinner.

My perfect plan wasn't working out so perfectly. I thought an intimate dinner at one of the nicest local black-owned restaurants would provide the best atmosphere for the parents to meet, but it was fast becoming a disaster. Paschal's Restaurant and Bar was one of my favorite soul food restaurants in Atlanta. It's one of the staples in Atlanta cuisine. The intimate setting makes it cozy and perfect for a first time meet. Fortunately, I knew the staff there and they always treated me and my family with respect, and knew that any commotion by my party would be handled.

Before things could get out of hand between my mom and Candace's parents, I took over. I knew no matter how rude my mom had become, my dad would support her publicly and deal with her privately once they got back home. "I don't understand the nature of your question," Candace's mom said immediately to my mom, while staring her straight in the eyes. It wasn't one of those friendly stares. She looked at my mom as if she wanted to beat her ass or spit in her face. My intervention was just in the nick of time. "Look, we're not here to figure out if you guys are gonna get along or not. We are here because Candace and I love each other, and we plan on getting married, with, or without, your approval. Whatever dislikes you all may have for one another, you better find a way to set aside your differences, because Candace and I aren't going anywhere, and you damn sure don't want us to keep your future grandchildren away from you," I said sternly, as if I were a parent handing out discipline. I could see in the corner of my eyes that my dad was proud of me for standing up to the situation. I didn't want any disrespect on either side. Candace's parents have always been kind to me, and they welcomed me into their family. I wanted my parents to do the same for Candace and her family. My eyes were almost fixated on my mom, while I talked, but I also glanced over at Candace to make sure she was okay. "I'm not insinuating anything. I'm just saying that a lot of illegal immigrants are coming to this country to take jobs away from Americans, and most of those jobs are usually taken from black people," my mother tried to say it under her breath, but it was loud enough for anyone within earshot to hear. "Well, if Americans really wanted those jobs, people from foreign countries who often don't even speak your English language, wouldn't have a chance to get them," Mrs. Joseph angrily responded to my mom. I knew I needed to put a stop to the back-and-forth banter before it got out of hand. "We're not here to check anybody's legal status. Nobody here works for INS. We're here to celebrate the union of two families and the addition of my future wife to my own family. The Josephs have been nothing but kind to me, and I expect my family to treat them kindly. That's all I'm going to say about that, and you all better find a way to get to know one another before the wedding," I said, before sitting down next to Candace. "You know I love you like crazy, right? But that love keeps increasing day by day, because you're such a great man," Candace whispered in my ear after I sat down. I loved my fiancée and I wanted to protect what we were building. "I'll drink to that," my father said, while raising his glass of water, trying to ease the tension. My dad was always the diplomat in the family. He loved my mother, but he also knew she could go overboard sometimes with her bullshit. I love my mom, but sometimes she's on some bullshit.

We managed to get through dinner without any disagreements. Of course, our food was new to the Joseph family because they hadn't explored soul cuisine since they'd been in this country. Mr. Joseph was also a diplomat in his own right, so to turn the environment back to normalcy, he asked, "Is collard green a staple when it comes to soul food?" My mom was more than eager to respond and brag about her culinary skills at the same, "It's not soul food if collard green is not included in the meal. The perfect amount of spice and seasoning has to be added to the fat back, in order for the flavor to stand out. You also can't overcook the collard green, because it won't taste right. In addition, we must include black-eyed peas as well to the meal." The Josephs listened intently, while savoring the collard greens. "The reason why I'm asking is because, no matter how different we think we are, the roots of our meals are mostly African. We also eat a lot of greens and black-eyed peas, just like the

African-Americans do. Our food may be presented differently, but we seem to eat pretty much the same things, and season our food almost the same way to give it that authentic African flavor," Mr. Joseph said. Mr. Joseph noted while the food may have been cooked differently, the ingredients were quite similar. After a while, he also felt he needed to address my mom's concerns and educate her about his status in this country, and the reason why so many immigrants move to America.

"I know not too many folks understand this about immigrants and the reasons why they are forced to move to America, but nobody really wants to leave their home country to migrate to a foreign country. That's like you leaving your hometown where you grew up to move somewhere else because you have limited opportunities in your hometown. You see, what America is doing to the black community here in America, they also practice in black countries overseas. All the drugs, the guns, and the criminal element you find in the black community here, are here by design. The racist system in place requires certain elements to work, in order for them to maintain this false sense of white supremacy. I don't know everything about American history, but I've read a lot about black history in this country. White supremacy is purported on lies and false histories about white people, which forces black people to have a false sense of inferiority. Of course, this doesn't apply to all black people, but a lot of black people actually feel that white people are better than them, because they don't know their true history and don't understand the false representation of white history," Mr. Joseph said, while intently focusing on my parents. "The reason why so many of our people are ignorant, it's because our black history is not part of the curriculum in the public school," my dad responded. "Who controls and funds your public schools? They do. Nobody's going to tell a glorified story about a group of people that makes them appear less than they have fooled the world into believing they are. White supremacy is a fallacy that's been around for hundreds of years. These fools have the nerve to tell the world Christopher Columbus discovered the entire world, where people already existed. And the weird thing about it, the entire world bought it. As a matter of fact, even African and Caribbean countries celebrate Columbus Day. A murderous terrorist who went around the world terrorizing indigenous people. It's a strong narrative and false propaganda that's going to take decades, perhaps centuries to erase out of the minds of not just black people, but also the billions of white people who believe that bullshit. Excuse my French," Mr. Joseph said. I looked around to see the looks on the women's faces as my dad and Mr. Joseph engaged in this intellectual conversation. Candace was proud that her dad was so knowledgeable, but more importantly, she was happy that her parents and mine had found a happy medium where they could engage in a fruitful conversation that benefitted everyone at the table. I couldn't hide my glee. I was happy they were getting along. At the end of the day, our common ground was our blackness, and we had to submerge the willful ignorance, in order to move forward.

PLANNING A WEDDING

Candace and I never officially had an engagement party, because we didn't have a lot of friends. After making it known to our family that we had gotten engaged, we wanted to put everything in place, so we could start planning our wedding. Candace was adamant about asking a couple of her cousins from New York to be part of the wedding. Her maid of honor was her best friend, Sandra, from high school, and she wanted three of her cousins to be bridesmaids in the wedding. Because we were planning a destination wedding, she needed to make sure only the financially responsible members of her family were invited. She didn't want any hiccups with anything, so she limited the numer of people she wanted to invite. As for myself, I knew I could rely on my immediate family members to attend, and my boy Darnell to be my best man. Darnell was my buddy from the military. We had grown close while serving, and over time, he became my best friend. Since we were having a destination wedding in the hot summer in the Caribbean, we wanted to keep everything light and white. There was no reason to bring dark colors into the hot Caribbean air.

Discussing the logistics with Candace was pretty easy, as I gave her the latitude to do anything that she wanted. I learned from my mother a long time ago, that a wedding is the coming out of a woman, and a dream day that no man can even fathom to understand. Since Candace was a lot more fiscally responsible than me, I didn't have to worry about her over-spending. I knew she would stick to the budget, so I told her whatever she wanted to have at the wedding, I was down. I also didn't want to leave her out there doing all the planning by herself, so I encourage her to get her friends involved, and even her mom, my mother, and my sister. Once she started talking about her wedding to family members, everyone offered to help and some people pledged financial assistance. Her dad offered a $5,000.00 gift she didn't see coming, and before we knew it, we had received pledges of monetary gifts of $20,000.00 from friends and family who wanted to help support the wedding. I cautioned her not to rely on promises of gifts, and to simply focus on what we could afford as a couple, so there would be no disappointment. "Babe, we should probably move forward with our plans to finance this wedding ourselves, so that we're not disappointed that people don't come through for us on our big day," I told her. "Say no more. That was my plan anyway. You know I don't ever rely on outside help to get anything done," she assured me. "I know, babe.

Maybe we can use the gift money that we might receive as part of a bigger down payment for our house," I casually suggested. "That was exactly my thought," she reiterated. That was the great thing about Candace, she was always practical. I never had to argue with her when it came to our finances. She was not a frivolous spender by any means.

After discussing our preliminary plans for the wedding, we started doing our research on available venues in Haiti. Candace and I looked at many different venues and the types of services they offered to wedding party, and settled on the Satama Hotel in Cap Haitien, which offered us a special all-inclusive package from Tuesday to Sunday for all of our guests. There were two reasons we chose this hotel. First, because Candace had never been to Cap Haitien and she said she wanted to explore that part of Haiti with her new husband. Send, we chose an all-inclusive hotel away from Port-Au-Prince, because we wanted our guests to spend very little to no extra money, when they came to our wedding. In addition, the resort offered all types of activities and ambiance that could be enjoyed by our guests during their stay. The resort is located less than two miles from the beach, with easy access to water sports and other aquatic activities offered by the hotel, in addition to complimentary transportation to the beach. We also went on their website to check out their ballroom, samples of foods, decorations, and pictures from past weddings, and felt comfortable with everything they had to offer. Candace's mother asked a friend of hers in Haiti to meet with the wedding planner at the hotel to make sure the food tasted as good as it looked, and the decorations were as nice as they looked in the pictures. The feedback was an astounding two thumbs up, as the place was a certified winner among all the other locations that we had explored online.

Candace and I had planned to arrive at the resort hotel the Sunday before the wedding, almost a week prior, so we could have enough time to make sure everything was going to be to our standards, liking and pleasure. Once we arrived, we were not disappointed. The resort was very clean, the staff was very friendly, professional, and accommodating, and the food we sampled in the dining room was addictive. I knew right away we had made the right decision by choosing this resort hotel, but more importantly, I was impressed with the setup of the location where the wedding ceremony was going to be held. The wedding planner decided to have two separate areas for the ceremony and the outdoor reception. The wedding ceremony itself was going to be set up on this huge open terrace that could accommodate all of our guests. There was a second oversized outdoor terrace where the actual reception was to be held and the food was to be served. It was a buffet-style reception dinner, which made it easier for my guests to select the foods of their choosing. The space wasn't so huge that we needed a bunch of servers running around to cater to our guests. A few servers were scheduled to work our wedding, and we were fine with that. The bar was perfectly situated and easily accessible to all of our guests. I could tell a lot of work went into the planning of everything, and I couldn't be more grateful to the hotel manager and the wedding coordinator.

We practically paid for everything within a few months before we went to Haiti. However, upon assessing the great length the staff had gone to satisfy us, I wanted to show my gratitude after the wedding. I had brought some extra money with me just in case, but I called my brother and asked him to bring a couple of hundred dollars extra for gratuities for the manager, the wedding planner, and their staff. It was my first time in Haiti, so why not? A few people from my family had decided they couldn't make it at the last minute because the expense was too high for some of them, but it didn't affect the cost and the outcome of the wedding. The resort had given us a set price for as many guests as we had requested, but they had no problem adjusting the price when I alerted them that a few people would not make it to the wedding.

While Candace and I were doing all this planning back home, July had crept up on us. We couldn't believe we had finally flown to Haiti to get married. I know that planning a wedding could be stressful, so I tried my best not to irritate Candace with unnecessary bullshit leading up to the wedding. I probably made love to her more than ever during the months leading up to our wedding, because making love is our peace, comfort, our best form of com-munication, in addition to just keeping the stress away, so we could have the best beginning of our married life together.

THE WEDDING

I can spend endless hours talking about specific details of our wedding because it was so magnificently perfect. I would just say that Kane made it easy for me to create my dream wedding because he never once fussed over anything that I requested during the planning process of our wedding. In addition, my wedding planner/coordinator was a great Haitian woman with an impeccable reputation and made every effort to keep her reputation intact throughout the planning process. I couldn't have asked for a better wedding coordinator. I had planned to walk down the aisle a completely happy and fulfilled woman, and it all came to fruition, thanks to my husband and all the people who came together for the most beautiful and important day in my life, behind the birth of my children.

Because of the hot sun in July in the Caribbean, I suggested that everyone should wear white to the weddings, because the entire wedding ceremony was taking place outdoors. The reception was in an open-air patio, as well as the dance floor, which was under a covered tent. I didn't want anybody sweating too much in their clothes. I wanted to make sure the heat was going to be reflected, not absorbed by their garment. While everyone was encouraged to wear white, it wasn't mandatory in order to attend the wedding. We didn't want to impose too much on our guests. They were doing enough flying all the way to Haiti to come to our wedding. We wanted everyone to show up to support us and enjoy their stay in Haiti at the same time. Most of our guests made use of the group discount rate offered by the hotel. A few people chose to stay elsewhere, but there were no problems with them attending the wedding. Some folks even stayed with family, while in Cap Haitien.

The Satama Hotel was nothing short of breathtaking and perfect for everything that Kane and I ever dreamed our wedding would be. Most of the guests arrived a couple of days prior to the wedding and were impressed upon arrival, because of the friendly and attentive staff that greeted them upon entry into the hotel lobby, in addition to the aesthetics of the hotel. The staff there was very accommodating in every sense of the word, and my guests felt very happy and comfortable almost instantly. The reception a person receives from the front desk receptionists at any hotel, usually dictates how their stay will be. My husband and I were treated like VIPs and honored guests of the hotel the entire time we were there. However, I was more impressed with the set-up. My eyes lit up when I saw the covered white chairs on both sides of the oversized terrace with an open pathway in the middle, which would be lit with lanterns that were lined up from the terrace door of the hotel, all the way up to the beautiful arch near the altar, where the bride and groom would meet the officiating minister for the wedding. The groomsmen and bridesmaids would stand on both sides of the aisle behind the lanterns, which would create a well-lit path for my husband and me as the honored couple, while we walked down the aisle, before the wedding party make their way to the front. The arrangements were amazing!

Finally, the day of the wedding had arrived and 6:00 PM was fast approaching. The day before, I met with the wedding party and we went over the positions we would on the terrace during the wedding ceremony with the groomsmen and the bridesmaids. The plan was to have them walk together, arm in arm, in the middle of the path toward the front, the groomsmen would single file to the left side to stand a couple of steps from the pulpit, and bridesmaids would single file to the right to stand in the front row a couple of steps from the pulpit before the bride and groom walked down the aisle. At the command of the officiating minister, they would be able to take their seats for the ceremony. The visuals were more than Kane and I expected. They also stationed a grand piano on the side, where the pianist would play the wedding theme song, as Kane and I walked down the aisle. Everything was well planned down to the minute details.

My hairdresser and makeup artist arrived promptly at 2:00 pm to get my hair and makeup ready for the big ceremony. My mind was at ease because, finally, I was going to marry the man of my dreams and my best friend. Kane and I would become one, once and for all. It's been a great journey learning how to love this man. While taking the longest shower of my life, I started reminiscing about all the good times that I've spent with Kane, and fantasized about the greater times ahead. I was the happiest woman there ever could be, and I had planned to make sure that Kane never regrets his decision to marry me. I love this man so much, I just wanted to get to the altar to say our vows and be done with it. The rest was just the cherry on top.

I knew everybody at the wedding was going to wear white, so I especially asked my bridesmaids to wear white linen spaghetti strap fitted dresses, which were accented with a white skinny belt that I found at this local boutique in Atlanta. The boutique owner, a beautiful sister in her mid-thirties, was more than accommodating when I told her that I loved the dresses so much and needed three of them in different sizes for my bridesmaids. All the bridesmaids were required to wear black shoes. Everyone was fitted before we left, and I carried the dresses with me to Haiti. The groomsmen kept it very simple. They wore white linen pants, white linen short-sleeved shirts with black shoes. My maid of honor was able to choose her own dress, and she didn't disappoint. She wore a white elegant ruffle trim, bow front high and low hem tube formal dress, exposing her beautiful shoulders and back, with a liner in the front and back, to make sure her entire butt was covered. My best friend has a banging body, so the strapless tube dress accentuated her every curve in the most stunning way. The Caribbean heat gave her the opportunity to show off her beautiful back. Everybody who was part of the wedding party looked great. However, not to be outdone at my own wedding, I wanted to wear something that would accentuate my curves as well, because only lord knows how long I was going to manage to keep this body, especially after giving birth. I threw caution to the wind and went all out. I wanted my husband to focus on me. I wore a gorgeous long-sleeve lace court train tulle mermaid cut dress that fit my body perfectly. I felt like a princess after I put the dress on. I knew the dress was perfect for me when I saw it the first time. I don't know if it's customary for the groom to see the bride's dress or not before the wedding, but I managed to get Kane to give me his opinion on 10 different dresses that I had in mind from this website, and I saw how his face lit up when he came across the particular dress that I chose, without his knowledge. All I needed was his consent. I never really had a weight problem, but I made every effort possible to keep my weight intact, so the dress would fit perfectly on my wedding day.

I knew my husband was going to look handsome in his suit, because Kane has always had a natural wholesome, clean, handsome face and beautiful presence. I couldn't wait to lay eyes on him. I had no idea he was going to be standing at the altar in a white fitted fine linen suit, white linen shirt, and gorgeous moccasin black shoes. I'm usually not a fan of men wearing moccasin shoes, but Kane managed to pull it off. My man looked sexy as hell, and I couldn't wait to marry him. The entire damn wedding party and the guests looked great in their white outfits. After my dad walked me down the aisle to deliver me to the altar, I glanced at our parents sitting in the front, my parents on the side of the bride at the end, and Kane's parents on the side of the groom at the end. I saw the glee in the faces of every one of our guests. I knew our blended family and friends had come together to witness and bless our union with their presence, and with the mindset that we were always going to be connected forever. It was at that moment I realized that Kane and I were going to be one forever, and I looked forward to our new beginning. I know my friends and family couldn't see my face because of the veil, but I'm sure my body language let them know that I appreciated their presence at my wedding. Here comes the bride...

CAN WE HAVE THE HONEYMOON BEFORE THE WEDDING?

I was already standing at the altar and making eye contact with friends and family when the pianist started harmonizing "Here Comes the Bride" with the piano keys. I turned to see Mr. Joseph walking down the aisle with Candace on his arm, making his way to deliver his beautiful daughter to me. Even in a wedding dress, Candace's walk was still sexy. One of the things I always found sexy about Candace was her walk. She's a little bowlegged, so her walk is out of this world. She and her dad strutted to the wedding symphonic tune, as I waited nervously to stand next to her. The entire wedding party stood up to welcome my queen. She was the most beautiful woman on that terrace.

"Oh my God!" was all I could say when I laid eyes on Candace at the altar. God saved her that day because I wanted to jump her bones. My baby looked good. She was the finest woman I knew at that moment, nothing short of a goddess. I can't even describe what went through my mind when she met me at the altar. I felt like I was the luckiest guy in the world. Everything about her was so perfect at that very moment. I took inventory of her curvaceous body in that white dress, and I almost developed a boner in front of everybody. The excitement wasn't so much about Candace's beauty, but more about her becoming my lovely wife. I had to turn and look into the crowd to regain self-control. My baby's smile shined brighter than ever, and I could read happiness all over her face. I spotted my mom sitting in the front row with teary eyes, but I knew they were tears of joy. The woman who stood before me that I was planning to dedicate my life to, was so much like, and also so different, from my mom at the same time. I wanted to take a moment to cherish my friends and family for coming down. I acknowledged them all with a wink. It was time, and I was ready.

The setting for our wedding was nothing less than breathtaking, magnificent, and extravagant. We received way more than we paid for. The entire wedding party looked great. I felt a little anxious, but in a good way. I don't know if anybody else ever felt that way on their wedding day, but I couldn't wait to make love to my wife. The reality of us becoming one was upon us, and I selfishly couldn't wait to whisk her away, just so I can have her to myself. Her flawless makeup looked natural, and the look in her eyes told me everything I needed to know about how she felt about me. I knew that Candace loved me with all her heart. However, there were a few more people in the audience who made me feel loved as well. I glanced over to see my mother's eyes filled with joy. When we locked eyes, she gave me that look of security and approval to let me know that she loved me as her son and she was completely fine with my choice to marry Candace. When I looked over to my dad, he had his fist pumped up to celebrate his son becoming a man. I saw pride in his face because he had accomplished his goal as a father to raise me into a man, and now a husband that will keep the family legacy alive. I wanted to make them proud.

The wedding ceremony itself was pretty brief, because we chose not to go through the entire longwinded shenanigans that usually take place at a traditional church wedding. The wedding officiant said a few words, and then asked God to bless our union, before we exchanged our vows. It seemed as if we were both impatiently waiting for the officiant to pronounce us husband and wife. We wanted the ceremony done and over with, so we could move to the festivities. Before the words, "You may kiss your bride," even escaped his mouth, I gave Candace the longest and most passionate kiss that I had ever given her publicly. She responded to my kiss with just as much passion. Some people joked that we could just go to our room upstairs to get the honeymoon started. But first, we had to go to the reception and get our party on.

My eyes were fixated on my wife's derriere, as we made our way to the reception hall after leaving the ceremony area of the hotel. I gave Candace another kiss, just because I needed to taste her lips one more time. The order of the procession into the reception hall was the groomsmen, the bridesmaids, our parents, and then us. Candace and I walked in as if we were at an R & B concert, dancing in strides, hand in hand to Mary J Blige's "My Everything," while blowing kisses to our guests. Midway through, I let my queen lead the way, so I can get a better view of her in that sexy dress from behind, as we walked toward the royal chairs that were set up as a throne for the king and queen of the hour. We got the formalities out of the way within the first half hour, because the people were there to enjoy themselves. The best man made his toast. Our parents gave us their blessing. Mr. Joseph, my new father-in-law, made a speech to caution me to be the leader of my family, and to make sure Candace and I kept the communication line open, and to always be there for one another. After all the formalities were over with, the wait staff came in with the food, which included traditional Haitian dishes, and American dishes that both sides of our family could enjoy. However, more people seemed to enjoy the Creole fish, sautéed in a tomato sauce with rice, than the Cajun stuffed chicken breasts with roasted potato, which was ordered mostly by my family. I saw a lot of people reaching over trying to get a taste of the fish from the people sitting next to them. My wife and I knew we wanted the fish, but I also tasted the chicken, and it was just as good.

After dinner, it was time for me to hold my wife close to my body and make her feel the love she was going to receive that night. We actually chose two songs to dance to, in order to cater to both sides of our family. I actually surprised Candace by choosing a Haitian song that I often heard her listening to. I was able to get the lyrics translated, and the song fell right in line with what I wanted to say to her. Klass was one of her favorite groups, and my wife loves herself some Haitian music, so I chose this song called "Map Marye," which means I'm getting married. I saw the shocked look on her face when she found out that I had chosen that song for our first dance. When I grabbed her hand to lead her to the dance floor, she asked, "How did you know that I love that song?" She wasn't ready for my answer, though, as I said, "You're my woman. It's my job to learn everything that you love, so I can keep you, and us, happy, for the rest of our lives. I received another beautiful kiss from my wife for my efforts while we were dancing. Just as I was about to walk back to our seats as the song was nearing its end, the DJ announced that there were actually two songs. Candace had chosen "I can't stop loving you" by Kem, as the second wedding song. She wanted to make sure my side of the family understood our love as well. We danced one more time, before asking the wedding party to join us on the dance floor. I'm truly in love with this woman.

As the reception died down, Candace and I walked around to thank all the people who showed up for our wedding. Their presence made the occasion special, and we were more than happy to share our most precious moment with them. Though we felt their presence was the best gift we could've received, some people still brought additional gifts of mostly cash to show their love and support. We were grateful and accepted all the gifts gracefully. While my mom decided to handle the actual gift items, Candace's mom collected the monetary gifts, which were mostly checks, and some cash. We left the reception hall knowing everything would be taken care of by our parents. We were happy that everything finally ended because we couldn't wait to get back to our room to end the night on an even higher vibration.

I'LL MAKE LOVE
TO YOU

Kane was the only man that I had ever truly made love to, and I wanted our wedding night to be special. He had no idea that I was wearing a two-piece sexy strapless bra and panty set under my wedding dress. I took notice of the eagerness and hunger in Kane's eyes. I knew he couldn't wait to devour me, while we were on the dance floor. I was just as thirsty and hungry for his love, but I was nonchalant about it. After all, my daddy was there, and I had to be a lady and act like Daddy's princess. As soon as we walked through the door of our suite, Kane pulled me toward him before I even had a chance to make it to the shower. I wanted to refresh with a shower before we did anything, even though I had on sexy undergarments to entice him. We started tearing each other's clothes off the second the door closed behind us. Kane stripped down to his underwear in less than 5 seconds. I stood there in my underwear and bra watching his bulge, and waiting to take him in my mouth. "I need to shower first," I told him as he reached for a handful of my ass cheeks. "Damn, babe, you're lucky I'm not making love to you in your wedding dress and me and my tux. I want this, babe," he said in the most begging and hungry way. Kane stared right at me, because he knew that I'm a clean freak, and there was no way I was gonna let him do anything to me without washing up first. Not that I wanted to ruin the moment or anything, but a sister has to feel clean. Suddenly, he whisked me off my feet and carried me to the shower. "I need to put up my hair," I told him before he turned on the water. This black hair can't afford to get wet. We have a week left to celebrate our honeymoon. "I know, babe. I got you," he said while handing me a scrunchie to hold my hair up in a bun. I don't know where he got it from, but he had it in his hand to give me right on time, along with a shower cap. My baby had me covered.

I put up my hair and put the shower cap over my head to step into the shower and Kane pulled me toward him for a kiss while he stood in front of the showerhead, protecting my hair from getting wet, as the water cascaded down our bodies. I could taste his smooth tongue twirling around mine in a French wrestle that felt so invigorating. He kissed me for the longest time as the hot water, that I knew he hated so much, pulsated on his back because he wanted to shield my hair from getting wet. At the most inopportune moments, Kane was always protective of me. That's why I love him so much. I ran my hands down Kane's back and across his chest as we made out in the shower. I wanted all of him inside me, but Kane had other plans. He leaned me back against the wall, bent down in a squatting position to set my right leg over his left shoulder, while his tongue invaded my heavenly abode. I watched the desire to please me on Kane's face with each stroke of his tongue against my clitoris. He looked up to see the look of pleasure on my face, which made him smirk a little. He reached for my ass with both hands, while I held on to this head for comfort, as he displayed his cunnilingus magic on my cooch. My grounded anchored leg trembled as Kane thrust his tongue in and out of me. "Yes, baby. Eat your kitty cat!" I screamed out. I didn't want to suffocate him, but I could feel the passion of his tongue pulling me out of my comfort zone. "You're making your kitty cat cum, baby. I'm cumming! Don't stop! Yes! Yes! Yes!" I kept screaming as Kane brought me to a state of euphoria that I had never experienced before. My entire body was shaking by the time Kane pulled his tongue back in his mouth.

My husband was standing there with a blood-filled, hardened johnson that deserved my attention. I had to regain my composure after the tremors I experience from having the most fulfilling climax in my lifetime. With the water flowing down Kane's back, which also served as a shield to keep me from getting wet, I kneeled down in front of him and took him into my mouth, swallowing his entire length and girth all at the same time. I was eager to please him. He was now my husband, and my job was to be the freak that he always wanted me to be. I wasn't overly experienced, but I did watch a couple of porno flicks before I came down to Haiti, and I was hoping to emulate some of the oral choreography that I had watched. I tried to deep-throat his johnson, but it was too long. I gagged a little bit and then backed off. I massaged his balls as I licked his shaft slowly. "Yes, babe, suck your shit," he moaned. I knew my skills would improve after watching those porno flicks, but I didn't think it would be that quick. I could tell that Kane was enjoying my performance, because his head was leaned back, as he prayed to the heavens for an early withdrawal. I took the head in my mouth and circulated the smoothness of my tongue all around it, while still massaging his balls. Kane's body tightened up, and I knew he was almost there. When he reached for my head, I knew he was about to explode in my mouth. His body started to shiver, and I didn't want him to lose his stride, so I sucked harder and allowed him to get it all out of his body and in my mouth for the first time in my life. The women I saw in the porno flicks took it all down their throats like champs, and I aimed to be my husband's champion that night. His body quivered while he released in my mouth. I saw the look of satisfaction and approval on his face when he pulled me up to kiss me.

Conserving water was the last thing on my mind, but Kane apparently wanted to act like an environmentalist, because we had been in the shower for a while. "Babe, the water's been running for a while. We should step out the shower and go finish this on the bed," he had the audacity to say to me after unloading in my mouth. "Hell no! I need you to take me right here and right now!" I told him very assertively and aggressively. "Well, damn! My bad! Come get it then," he said with a smile on his face, as if he appreciated my assertiveness. Once again, I leaned back against the wall holding on to the grab bar, with my left leg resting on the built-in soap dish, to give Kane full view of my throbbing kitty cat. I could see the voracity in his eyes as he grabbed his huge cock and inserted it inside my throbbing kitty cat. My legs almost felt numb with his penetration, but it was a good numbing feeling. He started stroking me slowly, while kissing me with the water still hitting his back. "I love you so much. I'm gonna take care of this kitty cat forever," he whispered to me. I could feel the sincerity in his every word. "Yes, baby, and this kitty cat's gonna take care of your needs forever. I was grinding on his johnson hard. I wanted to please him, but he was pleasing me more. I always enjoyed sex with my husband more when we were facing each other, caressing each other, kissing each other, and breathing on each other. That was always the height of my ecstasy. Kane had grown to learn my body, and he knew exactly what to do to make me succumb to his sexual prowess. While inside of me, Kane started sucking on my breast, which was my weakest erogenous zone. He sucked light and hard on my nipple, watching my face to read my reaction to his tongue and lips on my breasts. I preferred them to be licked gently when he's inside of me, because it doesn't keep me preoccupied with urge to climax, but that action itself was climatic, so I couldn't help myself. "Baby, I'm cumming again," I moaned to him. "I am, too, babe. Cum with me," he whispered. He gently stroked me and placed his tongue on my left breast to suck another nut out of me. Kane had a habit of grabbing my ass real tight whenever he was cumming, so I knew I had to let him have his. While I shook in ecstasy, he violently shook inside me and screamed out, "Damn, I love you!" I responded, "I love you, too.

THE FEEDBACK

Quite a few of our guests extended their stay beyond the day after the wedding. Most of them had never visited Haiti before, and all they knew about Haiti was the false narrative and propaganda told to them by the US media. However, the memorable experience of my guests in Haiti spread like wildfire through word of mouth and on their private social media pages, soon after the wedding was over. It seemed as if nobody wanted their vacation in Haiti to end, because there were so many adventures I had planned for them throughout the week. I wanted to make sure my guests have the most joyful time during every single activity scheduled. My wife's parents, Mr. and Mrs. Joseph, assisted us with some of the monuments our guests and ourselves needed to see while in Haiti. The scheduled tours for the week included visits to Palace Sans-Souci, the Citadel, Heroes of Vertieres monument, Cathedrale Notre Dame du Cap Haitien, the statue of Jean Jacques Dessalines, Cathedral Square, Fort Picolet, and more. We kept our guests entertained and busy for the most part because we wanted to make sure they would enjoy every dime spent to attend the wedding. Candace and I also toured most of these monuments for the first time. I was amazed when I started learning more and seeing with my own eyes the ruins and great monuments of this great nation that fought to end slavery.

The newbies to Haiti, including myself, couldn't stop raving about the country, because we saw a different image from what was being portrayed about Haiti in the US media. The amazing views of Haiti from the hotel were a constant topic of conversation for everyone. The rooms were opulent, the variety of different foods for breakfast, lunch, and dinner was great, and to top it off, the staff was the most courteous and kind that most of my family and friends had ever encountered. These were some of the feedback that I was getting from some of the remaining guests and other people who extended their stay a couple of more days after the wedding. They didn't have to convince me, because I saw the history and the eighth wonder of the world, The Citadel, for myself. The wedding planner and hotel manager catered to my wife's needs like she was a superstar vedette, but only without the singing skills, money or fame of Beyonce. The professionalism was excellent, as we used emails and WhatsApp as a mean of communication, while we were in the states to stay in touch with our wedding planner. I had peace of mind after meeting the staff when we first arrived, and taking a tour of the facilities of the hotel with my wife. Everything seemed effortless and the communication lines were always open whenever we needed our questions answered. I can't say that we didn't get our money's worth.

I made a request with the wedding planner to provide special romantic hue lighting on the dance floor for our first dance, and the manager had no problem honoring all of Candace's requests and mine. Since the DJ was a family member who flew down from the states, we didn't have to do too much planning around the type of music we wanted him to play at the reception. He knew exactly the kind of songs and music we wanted played at the wedding to satisfy both families. The music was a perfect blend of R & B, Hip Hop, Kompa, Afro beats, Reggae and a little Salsa and Merengue in between. Everyone had a great time. Of course, no black wedding is complete without the electric slide, so the electric slide was performed as well.

One of the things that I noticed the day after the wedding was the instant improved camaraderie between my parents and Candace's parents. My mom had let her guard down and started to accept the fact that we were now a blended family. She was also shocked to learn how Haitians had played a significant role in America from the inception of this country while visiting Haiti.

MARRIED AND FAMILY LIFE

Real family life for Kane and I began when we got back from Haiti, and were now a married couple. The reality of waking up next to Kane every day for the rest of our lives and putting up with each other's nuances and quirks was something that I looked forward to from the time I realized I was falling in love with him. We were officially a family, and I don't mean just me and Kane. I meant everyone, from my mother to his mother, to my father, his father, and brother and sister. Kane and I wanted our family to grow closer, and that's exactly what happened after we got married. We understood our union wasn't just about the two of us, because we eventually planned on having children, and we wanted our children to grow close and enjoy their grandparents from both sides. I made it my job to call Kane's mom at least once a week, just to check up on her and see how everything was going. His sister and I also developed a closer relationship, and she called me often to discuss relationship issues, career, and so on. His father always made his presence felt, whenever I was on the phone with his mom. I felt like I belonged to his family completely. My parents were a little different. They were the ones constantly calling to check on us every week. Kane developed a closer relationship with my father, but he loved the sweetness of my mother. We really enjoyed the chemistry among the family members, which helped to strengthen our own personal relationship and love for each other. I was blessed to have met Kane. I don't know what more I can say about my handsome and sweet husband.

I was no longer daddy's little princess. I was now officially Kane's queen, and I intended to honor the throne and wear my crown appropriately, and treat him as my king. From day one, Kane had always treated me like a queen, and I reciprocated by ensuring him he was my king, and will always be treated as such. Married life was great for the most part, for the first couple of years. We got a lot of our traveling out the way. We visited plenty of countries in Africa, the Caribbean, and Europe, while sharing Kane's one-bedroom apartment for the first six months of our marriage, in order to save money to purchase our first home together. We also grew even more admirable of each other, because we love and care about each other genuinely. There was nothing about Kane that I didn't love, and from his actions, there was nothing about me that he didn't love. We also spent as much time with our parents as possible. We tried as much as we could to alternate between my parents and his.

It was always a family affair when we got with the family. I never felt like an outsider around his family, and my family made sure he knew that he was one of us. Kane also grew to love my mother's black rice and "legume." Whenever we went to New York, Kane had the same request for a meal, and my mother always delivered. He loved black rice and legume so much, I had to force my mom to teach me how to make it for him.

Life for us was great for the most part, and then we started to get a little bored. Kane and I had a discussion about purchasing our first house, and the type of community and environment we wanted to raise our children. We settled on Gwinnett County, because the school system was pretty good there, and a lot of young black professionals were starting to migrate to Gwinnett County. We purchased a 4-bedroom house with 2.5 baths with a finished basement because Kane wanted his man cave. The house sat on almost an acre of land with an enclosed backyard, which was partly wooded. The only time the house ever felt like a home, was when our family visited with us. The feeling of emptiness would take over after each visit ended with our families. We used to look at the empty bedrooms and imagined our children running around. Let me correct that, I used to imagine our children running around and making noise in the house. Kane didn't seem to have a problem with just the two of us living in the house. However, after being in that big house with Kane for a couple of years, it was starting to feel

empty. It was time for us to share our love with another person, perhaps a little person that the two of us could create together. Kane
called it a bad case of baby fever because I wanted a mini-me, or a
mini-him, but I knew he was also looking forward to being a dad
himself, and both of our parents couldn't wait to become grandparents. They were always reminding us that it had been two years
since we got married, and it was time to work on having a baby. If
Mrs. Black had her way, she would teach me every detailed position
that I could possibly use during sex to get pregnant. I found it sweet
of her that we became so close that she could talk to me openly
about sex. My mom was also pushing the issue, but my dad always
told me to take my time, because there was no rush.

WE'RE PREGNANT

Not long after I had a conversation with my mom about my desire to become a mother, I learned my cycle was late, and I was not mad at all. I wanted to make sure that it wasn't just an abnormality with my period for a couple of days, so I said nothing to Kane. My husband and I were having sex like rabbits, and I knew there was a possibility that I could be pregnant in between time. For a little while after we got married, I was very careful and kept track of my ovulation schedule. I would tell Kane when he needed to have his pull-out game in full effect, so we could avoid a premature pregnancy. However, after a couple of years, it was time to do it for the baby. I wanted to get pregnant so badly, and I felt Kane was also ready for us to start a family. Everything in our lives was in order; we had purchased our first home, finances were up to par, as we had very little credit card debt, Kane and I had job security, our life insurance policies were enough to cover any accident, we had enough cash reserves to cover our expenses for a year, in case of an emergency, and we were in a position to afford a 529 college savings plan for our child or children, if one should come. We were ready!

I waited a couple of months before I finally took a pregnancy test to confirm my status. I was ecstatic when I saw the two bars, confirming that I was pregnant. Kane was still at work when I took the test at home. I had decided to take the day off work, after I learned I was pregnant. I was anxiously waiting for him to get home, so I could share the great news. I don't know if there was some kind of kinetic energy between Kane and I, but he walked through the door with a dozen roses and a bottle of red wine in hand, and told me how he appreciated and loved me, before I could even give him my usual hug and kiss when he got home. "Is that legumes that I smell," he asked as he walked through the kitchen. My legumes dish has a distinct smell because of the spices that I use to make it, and Kane knew right away he was in for a treat. "Yes, baby, I made you legumes and your favorite black rice," I told him. Kane and I didn't need a reason to celebrate each other. He was always kind and considerate, so I learned to be just as kind and as considerate as him. I love making his favorite meal for him just, but this day wasn't just because. I wanted the evening to be special, and I wanted to celebrate the possibility of having my first child with my husband. Normally, when we have a candlelight dinner, we always celebrate with a bottle of red wine, but we'd have to pass on that wine after I learned we were pregnant. It's not as if I told him earlier that day that I was going to cook his favorite meal, but somehow he felt the need to celebrate and show appreciation for his wife, so he brought home flowers and a bottle of wine. I'm a lucky girl. I count my blessings every day.

Kane was a clean freak, even though the table was already set for dinner and I was wearing his favorite lingerie, he wanted to take a shower before we ate. While I was downstairs putting the finishing touches on dinner, Kane came down wearing my favorite silk boxers and robe to sit down and have dinner with me. I could still see the twinkle in my husband's eyes after two years of marriage. His plate was set as we sat down to have dinner. Kane always ate his salad first, which basically consists of lettuce, tomatoes, and cucumber, and his favorite Italian dressing. We usually toast each other before we begin dinner, but I had to decline the drink, and he wondered why. "You're not gonna toast our love today, babe?" he asked. I look a little bit uncomfortable and suspicious, but I responded, "Sure. Can I do it with a glass of water?" He looked at me kind of funny because Kane knew how much I enjoy a glass of red wine. "Glass of water? This is your favorite wine that I bought for you," he sounded puzzled. "I know, babe, but I can't have that wine right now. Can we just wait until after dinner to talk about it?" I pleaded. He looked at me with concerns on his face, and asked, "Babe, are you okay? No, are we okay?" The suspense was too much to bear and I didn't want my husband to worry about something that was trivial. "Well, I wanted to wait until after dinner to tell you this..." He cut me off before I could finish my sentence. "Tell me what?" he asked anxiously. "Babe, we're pregnant," I revealed to him. He jumped out of his seat and ran toward me, and said, "Don't play with me, babe. Are you serious?" he questioned. "I am," I responded. "That's frigging great. I'm gonna be a dad?" "Yes, you are," I told him. Kane lifted me up from my chair and gave me the longest kiss and hug, and thanked me for being his wife and the mother of his future baby.

It was the most joyful dinner we ever had. Kane drank enough wine for the both of us in celebration. After dinner, he started contemplating plans for a boy, talking about, "I'm gonna have a mini-me, little Kane. I'm gonna teach him everything my dad taught me and more." I looked at the glee in his eyes, and didn't want to rain on his parade. I let him have his moment about his supposed son, but I also had to remind him that the baby could be a girl. "Babe, what if we have a daughter instead?" I asked him. "That's even better. She's gonna be daddy's little girl. It doesn't matter to me. I want our child to be healthy. I actually like the idea of daddy's princess. I dig it," he said. I didn't anticipate that my husband would be as happy as he was, but I realized how blessed I was to have such a husband. He never stopped surprising me with his reaction to every situation. "Babe, should we tell our parents now, or should we wait until after the first trimester?" he asked. Boy, how you know I'm not in my first trimester already?" I asked him. He smiled, turned to me, and said, "I know you don't think I pay attention, but I do. I know you didn't have your period last month." "How did you know?" I asked. "Babe, your mood changes every time you're on your peri-od. It's not anything I can't handle, but you're always more on the edge when you have your period. I took notice of it early on in our relationship, and I adjusted accordingly," he told me. This man had to be heaven-sent because he paid attention to my every quirks and every need. "I'm glad that you've always been so attentive. It makes loving you so easy. I appreciate you, Kane Black. I love you and I'm lucky that you're my husband," I told him. "I love you just as much and appreciate you more. We decided that we would wait until after the first trimester to tell our parents that we were pregnant.

We couldn't let the night go by without celebrating our future child. Kane made love to me all night that night, but he was espe-cially gentle, because this fool didn't want his penis to hit the child's head. I couldn't stop laughing when he said, "I'm only gonna give you half of what you normally get, because I don't want my child to come out with knots on their head. He was dead serious, too. "Boy, you're crazy. The baby's not even formed yet. How can you hit his/her head?" I said to him. "Babe, I'm just trying to be careful. I want us to have a healthy, baby, not some brain-damaged baby, because my Johnson was hitting him in the head," he said curiously enough in a serious tone. He also didn't want to be on top of me, so he wouldn't crush the baby. That night was the biggest laugh of my life until we both learned more about sex during the pregnancy. Of course, any medical advice that I needed, I went straight to my mom, and his mom.

SPREADING THE GREAT NEWS

After learning that I was pregnant, Kane and I scheduled quite a few visits with my OBGYN, to make sure we were doing everything possible in our power to make sure we have a healthy child and delivery. We also told our parents about the pregnancy, once we got beyond the first trimester. My mother couldn't wait to be a grandmother, and my dad couldn't wait to have a grandson. I don't know what it is with these men and their sons, and grandsons when they don't have a son of their own. As much as I've seen the danger black boys are facing in society on a daily basis, I wasn't sure if having a son in this current environment was the best thing for us. Black boys and black men are becoming an endangered species. I wanted a healthy, baby, but I also didn't want to have a child that I would have to bury, because of racism and other people's prejudices and stereotypes against him. The order of family is that the children are supposed to bury their parents, once the parents have lived their best lives. However, that hasn't been the case for many black children lately. From George Floyd, Tony McDade, Philando Castile, Mike Brown, Terrence Crutcher, David Felix, Alton Sterling, Oscar Grant, and Freddy Gray to Trayvon Martin, and 11 year-old, Tamir Rice, and many other victims, black men and black boys are becoming prey for these civilian and police predators who don't value black lives. Not to say that black girls and black women aren't also endangered, because Sandra Bland, Breonna Taylor, Rekia Boyd, and so many others were unjustly killed by police as well. During the first eight months of the year 2020, police murdered 164 black people. Fatal police shootings of unarmed black people in America are three times as high as their white counterparts, simply due to racism, stereotypes, and prejudices. Of course, I worried about the safety and livelihood of a daughter as well, but the probability of black girls and women getting killed by police is not as great as that of black men and boys. I didn't want to have to worry about burying any child of mine, however, any black couple or black woman birthing a son nowadays, knows that their son is facing the greatest risk and possibility of death in this volatile environment at the hands of police and racist civilians. I knew that Kane would be the best father in the world, and he would protect his family with his life, but I seriously worried about having a son. It weighed heavily on my mind that my son could become a victim for no reason. I had seen firsthand what happened to my own husband during an interaction with a cop.

Kane's mom was more excited about just becoming a grand-mother. She was truly happy for us. She didn't really care if we had a boy or a girl. She just wanted a grandbaby. His dad was also happy that Kane was creating his own legacy. As the baby developed in my stomach, both sides of the family grew closer. My mother and father-in-law called me almost every day to check on the progress of the baby, and so did my own parents. My mom, especially, nagged me to death, because she wished she was closer to me to help any way that she could. It wasn't until my second visit to the doctor, after my first trimester, that I discovered I was carrying twins. The ultrasound revealed a second baby. Kane was ecstatic when he found out we were having twins. Of course, we ran our mouths to the extended family, because we knew we might need the assistance of the grandparents during the first few weeks after delivery. Kane and I opted not to learn the sex of the babies, because we wanted the element of surprise, and we wanted to love our children uncon-ditionally, no matter what their sex was.

The nine months flew by very quickly, and before we knew it, Kane and I found ourselves parents of handsome twin boys. Kane had gotten his wish twice. I was happy that my boys came out healthy. All the grandparents flew down the day that they found out I went into labor. I had the love and support of my entire family while I was in the hospital. My boys came into the world in an en-vironment filled with love. The entire staff at the Northside Gwinnett-Women's Center was great during my delivery and stay at the hospital. The delivery went on without a hitch. I was able to take my bundles of joy home a couple of days after giving birth to them in the hospital. I was grateful that my family came down to Atlanta to help Kane and me get adjusted to parenthood. Kane's mom spent four weeks with us, but his dad had to go back after a couple of weeks, because he didn't have confidence that Kane's brother could keep his business afloat by himself while he was gone. Kane's mom had more trust in Kane's sister to help keep her hair salon organized. My mom stayed with me for six weeks, because she worried as a new and inexperienced mom, it would be too difficult to manage twin babies. My dad stayed a couple of weeks, because he had to go back to work. We had plenty of room for the entire family. While the grandparents were there, Kane and I barely held our children. We were lucky to have two babies, because our parents, each took one of the babies, and were constantly holding and spoiling the crap out of them during their entire stay. Purchasing a 4-bedroom house was probably the best thing that we could've ever done, because we had plenty of space for everyone to feel comfortable.

My babies' nursery was completely set up by the time I arrived home from the hospital, thanks to my husband and parents. I really didn't have to lift a finger for six weeks while the grandparents were there. They made the transition into parenting very easy and comfortable for me. I did spend time with the kids whenever they needed nursing. Kane and I had an entire village to lean on, as it related to the care of our children.

FAMILY LIFE

The boys were growing pretty quickly right before our eyes. At first, I wanted to name one of our sons after me, you know the junior that most men brag that they want? However, after carefully thinking about the situation, I decided to be fair. I couldn't name one child junior, while the other one would question how the decision was made to only show that much love to only one twin. Instead, I named the oldest one Toussaint Nkrumah Lumumba Black and the other Dessalines Malcom Xavier Black. I wanted their names to have historical significance. I appreciate my wife, because she's also selfless in her own way. I knew my wife would entrust me with any decision regarding our family. In order for me to be a great man or husband, I always have to put the needs of my wife and children first. That's the most important lesson my dad taught me. I will carry that lesson with me through many generations, if I'm fortunate enough to see my grandchildren, and great grandchildren.

Family life as we knew it was great. Candace and I were happy to be parents, and the boys always came first. When we were babies, my mom stayed home with me and my siblings until we were old enough to attend kindergarten. I wanted my own children to have the same experience. I was never a proponent of daycare, because it would give my children more opportunities to be exposed to germs carried by other children. So, I asked my wife to stay home with them until they were ready for kindergarten. Candace and I usually caught breaks from the boys during the summer when our parents came down to spend time with us and their grandchildren. My brother and sister came to Atlanta whenever time permitted, but it was more about exploring the city than it was about spending time with Candace, the boys, and me. I'm not tripping, though, because they were young and young people are all about themselves nowadays. Still, we were always happy to see them, and we always made them feel at home when they came to Atlanta. Not to say they didn't spend any time with us, but at night, they were nowhere to be found. The nightlife in Atlanta was difficult for them to resist.

As the boys got older, Candace and I would drop them off in New York at her parents' house for a couple of weeks during the summer breaks, and her parents would drop them off to my parents' house in Boston, so they could stay with my parents for another two weeks. Candace and I had an entire month to ourselves to do whatever we wanted to do while the kids were away. Staying with our parents also gave the boys the opportunity to develop closer relationships with their grandparents, and my siblings. My sister adored the twins. From what I heard, my brother used the twins to mack girls whenever possible, because they were so darn cute, and they made him look like the caring uncle. We had developed a system that worked for everybody. Our boys got to experience life in Boston and New York with their grandparents, uncle, and aunt, as well as Georgia with us. Candace and I would go on vacation during the summer when the children were away, and we'd get our freak on around the entire house without any restrictions for an entire month. We also planned family vacations with our boys, once they returned home from Boston and New York. We always made it a point to stop at one of the amusement parks on the way for at least one day, on our way to New York with the boys, and on our way back to Atlanta after picking them up from Candace's parents' house. Every year the boys chose the park or beach of their choice. We had plenty to choose from between Georgia and New York. The National Museum of African-American History and Culture in Washington DC was a mandatory visit the first time we took the boys to New York. Kings Dominion was a favorite, as well as Busch Gardens, Water Country, and Splashdown Water Park all in Virginia. One time we decided to go to Six Flags in New Jersey, and other times we went to Wet and Wild Emerald Pointe Water Park in Greensboro, North Carolina, Myrtle Beach in South Carolina, and so many other places, to give our boys the experience of a lifetime. We never took the boys to Disney. We were planning on taking them the summer of 2020, but Covid-19 hit, and we were forced to quarantine during the pandemic. Being cooped up in the house for so long with the children was driving us crazy. It took some convincing from my wife, but I finally agreed to take the kids to the park for a family picnic, with the understanding that they would wear their face-mask and keep six feet away from anyone else who might be at the park.

JUST ANOTHER DAY AT THE PARK?

After loading up our late model Infinity QX60, SUV, the children, myself and my wife hopped in the car and headed straight to Lenora Park in Snellville, GA, as a family, for some much needed reprieve, after being in the house for all these months. It was a warm sunny day, so naturally, there were many other people and other families at the park and a few joggers enjoying the nice weather as well. My wife and I chose a spot that was a little secluded from the crowd, because of my concern and worries about the Coronavirus, which was always at the forefront of my mind. Social distancing was a must, and I made sure our picnic area wasn't heavily trafficked by the other people in the park. After setting an oversized blanket on the grass and a one-sided see-through netted tent for privacy, and to keep the mosquitoes away, my wife set her picnic basket down, and pulled out a plate of fresh cut-up fruits to offer our two sons and myself something to snack on. The two boys were more anxious about running free, wandering the park, and acting like normal children, more than anything. "Listen, I don't want you two running around and playing too far from here, you hear me? Make sure you keep your mask on, and stay where I can see you at all times," my wife warned the boys, while she and I got comfortable on the blanket. "Don't make me leave this park early, because y'all don't know how to act. You better listen to your mom. The minute you two get out of my sight, we're outta here," I warned my sons. "We're just gonna play tag and race each other, Daddy," said Toussaint. Dessalines shook his head in agreement to back up his brother. The two boys had been inseparable since birth. Their genetic makeup was too identical sometimes for me to even tell them apart. The boys knew that as well, and they had played many tricks on me and my wife in the past, but over time, I was able to do a better job telling them apart and put a stop to the games they used to play on me when they were younger. My wife was especially skilled way more than me when it came to telling the boys apart. The one identifier on Toussaint was a small birthmark on his lower back, and I had to pull up his shirt to figure out whom I was talking to at times. My wife wasn't easily fooled when it came to the boys. They couldn't trick her like they tricked me. She knew her boys more than they knew themselves, and she understood that Toussaint was the mischievous of the two, and also the leader. Dessalines would do anything his brother told him to do. The boys loved one another, and they were always together. Dressing alike was par for the course, and it benefitted those boys in more ways than one. Toussaint was strong in science, but his attention span in math class at school was short. Dessalines was the math genius, as well as science, but there had been plenty of times when Dessalines was responsible for the math work that Toussaint handed in to his teacher. Those boys had a lot of tricks up their sleeves, but Toussaint was often the mastermind behind those tricks. Boys will be boys. What can I say? Sometimes I saw a lot of myself in my boys, and I would smile to myself with pride, and be thankful for my children and my wife.

Ever since my sons were born, they've been watching football with me, and in the process, developed an affinity for the game. After their fifth birthday, I had no choice but to sign them up for Pop Warner football at the Youth Athletic League at Bethesda Park. Toussaint was the hitter, so he played defense, while Dessalines was more on the offensive end playing receiver. That day, Toussaint carried the leather football in plain sight, as the two boys took off about twenty yards away from where we were lying down, so they could throw the football back and forth to one another. Toussaint remained dedicated to his favorite sport as he got older, while Dessalines own affinity for the sport waned in comparison, as he grew a little older and taller. Dessalines became a basketball fanatic, and his side of the wall in the bedroom he shared with his brother was covered with posters of LeBron James, Damian Lillard, and Steph Curry, his three favorite players. Toussaint's favorite player was Julio Jones from the Atlanta Falcons and Russell Wilson from the

Seattle Seahawks. Spending time with my family was essential to developing the close bond that we shared. My family was my pride and joy. While my wife and I were in the tent, I was laying on my stomach so she could rub my back, while looking up intermittently at the boys to make sure they were safe in between massage strokes. I was feeling great and relaxed with my wife's hands running all over my back, so I might have been distracted a little from the boys. She was always great at back massages, and I enjoyed every minute of her expulsing the stress out of my body. "You know, baby? I'm so proud of you as a man and father. I love and appreciate everything you do for our family. My boys and I are lucky to have a husband and father like you," my wife confessed to me. "Baby, it's my duty as a man to make sure my family is good. What kind of husband and father would I be, if I didn't do my best to make sure my family is good? I love you and the boys more than life itself," I told my wife.

All of a sudden, I heard two bangs that sounded like gunshots, followed by commotion and a stampede as the crowd ran out the park. "They shot them," we could hear one lady scream in horror, as she ran away from the commotion. My first impulse was to run out of the tent to get to my boys. "Please go find our boys," my horrified wife pleaded with me, as the stampede of people blocked our view from where the boys were playing. We had only taken our eyes off them for about one minute, while we engaged in a confession of our love for our family and each other. I stood up and ran toward the crowd to go find the boys, so my wife could have peace of mind. "Toussaint! Dessalines!" I screamed while I ran 20 yards toward the spot they were playing. As I approached the crowd, I could see two bodies lying on the ground. There was a black woman who identified herself as a nurse, doing her damnedest to try to give CPR to Toussaint, as his body was still convulsing on the ground in a pool of blood. I knew it had to be my boys, because I could identify them from a short distance through the blood-soaked clothing that they wore when we left the house. I fell to my knees upon reaching Dessalines. His body was lifeless. Dead. Unalive. Gone! "Move away from the man, ma'am," the shooting officer commanded to the lady giving CPR to my other son. "Put your hands up!" he continued to scream at the two bodies lying on the floor. It was obvious one of the bodies was lifeless. "Why did you shoot them? They're just kids playing cowboys and Indians," the lady managed to utter through sobs, tears, and sorrow. I tried to pick up Dessalines body, but the cop pointed his gun at me, and commanded me to put my hands up, which I obliged, after slowly putting my son down. I was fuming inside and I wanted to charge him at that very moment. I didn't care that he had a gun, but something came over me, and I caught a deep breath, while staring him dead in the eyes. He was uncomfortable and scared at the same time. I had to contain myself because my wife couldn't afford to lose her entire family in one day. I could've easily wrapped my hands around his neck and wrung the last breath out of him, because I saw the cowardice in his eyes. I had seen that look before during my tours in Iraq and Afghanistan when I faced adversaries who were killing innocent children in the name of Allah. I also could've easily walked to my car to retrieve my loaded gun and let a few slugs into this coward, but I couldn't destroy my wife like that. I had to be there for her. I wanted to stick around, and I wanted her to partake in the sweet victory of revenge, along with me. I had to be more calculated than a two-dollar cowardice cop who was so afraid of two young black boys that he had to murder them in public to submerge his insecurities.

"You're interfering with a police investigation," the killer cop told me after shooting my son. "You just killed my fucking son!" I yelled at him. The mostly white crowd looked on, as my devastated wife made her way to us, screaming hysterically, because as a mother, she could tell from a distance that her two babies had been shot down. By then, more gang members in blue had arrived, and they started creating a barrier with their yellow tape to prevent me and my wife access to our son. The nurse couldn't save Toussaint. Both of my sons were dead. In my mind, all I could think was, someone had to pay for this, and it wasn't going to happen through the court system, and some stupid monetary settlement. It was going to be a life for a life. I followed the Tamir Rice case in Cleveland, and it was up to me to change the outcome for my sons. Fuck the system! Fuck the justice department. Fuck Benjamin Crump! And Fuck the police! While I stood there consoling my wife who was sobbing, all I could do was whisper in her ear, "I'm gonna get him. I promise you. Our sons will not die in vain." I was contemplating the many ways I was going to torture this cop before I rip his fucking heart out of his chest. I made sure I looked at the name on his badge to remember the correct spelling and his badge number. I memorized it, just like I memorized the horrendous death of my sons at the hand of this filth. Vengeance was going to be mine, and there was nothing anybody was going to do about it.

The hysterics went to the next level once Dessalines was confirmed dead and placed in a body bag by the coroners. Meanwhile, the nurse who was trying to save Dessalines was not just angry, hysterical, and sobbing anymore, she was totally discombobulated. "That could've been one of my sons," she uttered through sobs with eyes full of tears, while talking to me. She was pained by what happened, but more importantly, she felt dejected, because she knew we were going to get railroaded by the system after the incident, because justice may never come. Everybody seemed to have known that, but not me, though. I knew I wasn't going to wait on this racist system to provide me the peace of mind that I needed to justify my sons' deaths. This was going to be a next-level fight that I started planning in my head against the system, and I intended to win on every level. My military training gave me insight into the enemy, and I knew he would be an easy target. However, I also had to consider the collateral damage that was to come with vengeance for my sons.

My calm demeanor frightened the killer cop who murdered my two sons. I could see fear in his eyes, as he stood there talking to the investigators, trying to concoct a fictitious story of defense, probably involving the usual " I feared for my life" bullshit that they're trained by the academy to use, whenever they unjustly murder black people. I was ready for it, and the usual nonsensical vitriol used by cops to demonize black victims posthumously. My sons were only eleven years old, but I was certain those racists would be creative enough to find ways to criminalize them in their death. I didn't want to cause a scene, so I slid out of the park, and went to sit in my car to make sure I kept my eyes on the killer cop the entire way. I already knew the procedures, after one of these bastards kill an innocent person. Granted my sons were a little taller than usual for their age, standing at 5'10, but their scrawny bodies hadn't fully developed yet. They looked like normal kids, and their baby faces confirmed it. I was mad, sad, angry, revengeful, and filled with so many emotions at the park, I just had to walk away to compose myself, so I could figure out how to handle the deaths of my sons. It wasn't fair for me to leave my wife grieving alone, and to face the investigators, but no one knows me as well as my wife, and nobody knows her as much as I do. My wife is strong, and I knew she'd want me to do something about the death of our sons. We could always read each other's minds, and there was no better time for our thoughts to be fluid and in unison than at that moment.

I sat in the car for almost an hour, while the police investigators conducted their investigation. My wife knew where I was, because I alerted her before walking away. This killer bastard was being handled with gloves, as he was driven to the hospital to get himself checked, after killing my two sons. I was hot on their trail. I tried to stay as inconspicuous as possible, as I followed them to the hospital. My job wouldn't be complete, if I didn't find out where this cop lived. I was going to be his worst nightmare for the next few weeks, but without him knowing it. It took a while for him to emerge from the hospital, but when he did, accompanied by two cops, I was on their trail again. I followed him until he was dropped off at home, minus his service revolver. I was no fool. Just because this guy didn't have his service revolver with him, it didn't mean he didn't own other guns. After all, this was Georgia. My adrenaline was flowing and I wanted to get rid of the bastard as soon as the opportunity presented itself, but I thought about my wife grieving her entire family without my support. I started to recalibrate my mind and shifted my focus to a better plan. This man needed to suffer the consequences of murdering two young boys for no reason. I had to be more calculating than ever. I knew it would be a while before the doctored version of the footage from the body-cam the cowardice cop wore when he murdered my son would be released. These police departments don't like culpability, because it brings more liability. I also didn't want to become a victim of circumstance. The circumstance of my sons' deaths would instantly draw attention to me, had I eliminated this coward cop right away. I needed to beat them at their own game, so I chilled. I went home to my wife to console her.

THE BEREAVEMENT PROCESS

I really didn't know what to say to my wife when I walked through the door that evening. I was angry, and felt powerless at the same time. As a man, I'm supposed to be the protector of my family. I failed my two boys. I needed to do something that could bring comfort to my wife, to make her feel that our sons didn't die in vain. I also understood that my wife was way too intelligent to believe that a reckless reaction to our sons' death would help alleviate any pain we were feeling, or ease the bereavement process. I looked around, but I didn't see my wife in her favorite spot on the couch when I walked into the living room. I wandered throughout the house looking for her. I figured she might've been in the bedroom still balling and crying from the pain of almost witnessing the deaths of two beautiful young boys she brought into this world, but instead, I found my wife downstairs in the basement rummaging through my collection of guns that I kept in a locked safe in my private man cave. Normally, she would not barge into the man cave, because she knew it was my private place of respite from the family, but I understood the reason she was in there. My wife was an emotional wreck. I had given her the combination code, in case of emergencies, and this was definitely an emergency. My wife and I were gun enthusiasts and we spent a lot of our pastime at the shooting range, especially before the boys were born. I always made sure that my wife knew how to defend herself, and carrying a gun every day was part of the process. We had gotten our license to carry right after we graduated from college. However, my wife didn't know which handgun would be the easiest to handle, in order to carry whatever mission was in her head at the moment. I could tell that vengeance was on her mind from her demeanor, and the sinister look on her face. She wasn't even crying anymore. It was just pure anger, and her eyes dictated she wanted vigilante justice. I had never seen that side of her since we'd been together, but I was glad to see that my wife wasn't going to hold me back from doing something about my sons' deaths.

"Babe, are you okay," I calmly asked, while approaching her for an embrace. "Of course, I'm not okay. A cop just murdered our sons. The two people we love the most in this world. No, I'm not okay. I want to do something about it. No, we need to do something about it. We're not going to take this shit sitting down. This motherfucker has to pay," she said with anger, disappointment, and sadness in her voice. I could feel my wife's pain, because I was agonizing over the same thing. "Let's calm down and figure out a proper and satisfying way to handle this. We know the media is gonna be all over this case for weeks to come, so we're gonna have to show patience, before we can do anything. I'm gonna need you to go through the motions, just like everybody else. We're gonna act as forgiven as black people can be, but only you and I are gonna know what the real plans are," I told my wife. "I don't know how you can be so calm, cool, and collected after our children were murdered, but I guess one of us has to have the composure to see the situation through," she told me as tears flooded her eyes. I knew I needed to be strong for my wife. I had to allow her the emotional space to grieve. I wanted her to know that I would be there to support her all the way through. The boys were already dead, and we couldn't bring them back, so that's a reality we had to get comfortable with. However, I reiterated clearly to her that justice and vengeance will be ours. Still, I didn't want to make false promises to my wife. I needed to figure out a way to get the well-deserved justice that we wanted.

In the midst of consoling my wife, I realized we had forgotten to alert other family members about the death of our sons, before they suffered a heart attack, while hearing about it on the news. Our parents were very close to the boys, and we had better deliver the bad news to them quickly, before the media painted whatever picture they wanted of our boys to justify their murder. While words about the murder of our sons were rapidly spreading on social media and the local news, the narratives were very different from both. Social media was more about factual information posted by witnesses who were at the park when the shooting happened, while the mainstream local media was trying to fabricate a scenario where the police officer had no way to justify whether my sons were playing with toy guns or real weapons. We'd always made it a point to get our boys toy guns with the bright orange hue on the muzzle, so there's no mistaking them for real guns because they were black boys. Still, the local media was reporting that two weapons were found at the scene, without actually showing the weapons to the public. We didn't want the national news to cover the story before our family members got wind of it. I decided to tell my wife that I was going to call my parents and siblings to inform them about the devastation we were experiencing and also asked her to call her parents to let them know what happened. We didn't want our own family to be influenced by the demonization of our boys by the media.

As expected, my mom and my sister were hysterical and devastated at the same time. My brother Jeff was the ultimate activist. He wanted all the details, so that he could galvanize a movement for justice on his social media page. My sons were the only grandchildren in my family, and the only nephews my siblings had. They were also the sole grandchildren on my wife's side as well. My dad was calm more than anything. Our conversation was a little different. He was trying to get me focused and tried his best to remind me of my role as the head of my family. "You must stay strong for your wife, but at the same time, you have to defend your family. We already understand how the justice system works, so we have to do everything in our power to get justice for the boys. Your mother and I will be down there as soon as we can to help you sort out the situation, so you can focus on what you have to do. You know what I mean?" my dad said. I understood exactly what he meant. My dad had always protected his family. It didn't matter if it was the police or one of those wannabe gangsters around the way who threatened our livelihood. My dad always went toe to toe with the system and people who wanted to hurt his family. From the time I got married and became a father, my dad made it clear to me that nobody should ever be more important to me than my own wife and children, not even him and my mother. He sent me out in the world prepared to be a dad and husband, and he expected no less from me.

We didn't have much time for grief, because my family was organizing for justice and revenge. We knew getting an indictment on the killer cop from a grand jury in Gwinnett County was slim to none, because more than likely the grand jurors would be all white, and without a sense of justice or empathy for the murder of two young black boys at the hands of a white police officer. We'd seen it in Cleveland with Tamir Rice, when he was murdered by a white officer while playing with a toy gun, with no questions asked, as the cop pulled up to the scene. That case had set the precedence for what would be our expectations. We also knew that the killer cop was rehired in a different town to work as a law enforcement officer, because they didn't revoke his certification as a peace officer. We had to get ready for all of it. I just knew that there was no way I was going to allow my boys to die in vain, even if my own life would be in jeopardy while seeking justice and avenging theirs.

THE FAMILY

I was numb to the pain of my sons' deaths. We needed to make arrangements for their funeral, but more importantly, we needed to make sure we got justice for our sons. My in-laws, along with my husband's brother and sister flew in from Boston two days after receiving the news from Kane. My parents came a day later from New York. We were in full effect and ready to hash out a plan for justice for our sons. "If this bastard is not arrested and taken to jail, I'm gonna make sure I bury him six feet under with my hands!" my husband screamed in the middle of the living room while the family gathered. Kane was as pissed as I have ever seen him. I was right there with him. All hands on deck. "Wait a minute now, we have to be strategic on how we move on this," said Mr. Black, Kane's dad. "We're not going to be losers all around in this. I already lost my grandsons, I'm not ready to lose my son to the system as well," Mr. Black continued to reason. "Dad, if I can't protect and defend my family, what's the point of living?" Kane questioned. Everyone looked on in silence, because Kane needed that moment to release the frustration he was dealing with. We all wanted to hear what he had to say. "You're right, big bro. Dad always taught us his job was to always protect his family," said Cynthia, Kane's sister, riling him up. "My job is to galvanize as many people on social media as possible, to take to the streets to start the biggest protest in the history of this country," said Jeff. "We all have a role to play here, but the main goal is to be victorious when the dust settles. We can't afford to have any more casualties. The system always wins, so we must do everything in our power as a family to make sure we are victorious against the system, and to set the precedence, so that another black family won't go through what we are facing right now. It's time to teach them a lesson," said Mrs. Black. "Victorious indeed. I don't know how you all are planning your victory, but in the Joseph family, we call on our ancestors before we go into battle, and we always win," my father said, as my mom shook her head in agreement. "What do you mean?" Mr. Black asked. "Have you ever read a book about the Haitian Revolution," my father asked Mr. Black. "Actually, no. I've heard about the Haitian Revolution, but it was never taught to us in school in the States," Mr. Black answered. "Well, we are all family here. My daughter is married to your son, and we are here because our grandsons were murdered by a scumbag cop who didn't value his life, right? My job as the patriarch of my family, and grandfather to those boys, is to make sure the person who killed them pays with his life. We don't get on our knees and pray to Jesus for an answer in this family. Nope, that's that slave mentality bullshit, forgive and forget that some African-Americans do. Malcolm X and Dr. King were polar opposites, as it relates to their approach and philosophy in the fight for human rights, but they were both assassinated. These people have never valued our lives, and it's about time they get a taste of their own medicine. I have revolutionary blood, and I know my history. We fight fire with fire," my father said, sounding as Haitian as he has ever sounded since I've been born, because his thirst for revenge was at the boiling point, bringing out his thick Haitian accent. When Haitians lose their cool, you better get ready for the wrath. My dad was taking the conversation to a whole different level that Kane's mom and dad weren't prepared for. They had this dumbfounded look on their faces. "I read about the Vodou ceremony that took place before the Haitian Revolution began. That's right. We need to go back to our roots and make these motherfuckers pay," Cynthia said, all hyped up, without a care in the world that she had just cussed in front of all the elders in the room. At least one person from Kane's family understood where my father was coming from. My mom stayed quiet the entire time, because she understood exactly what my dad was talking about, and what he was capable of under duress. "If we don't protect our children and our family, who will?" my mother blurted out. Mr. and Mrs. Black, along with Jeff, Cynthia, myself and Kane shook our heads in agreement. "It's settled then, we've all agreed it's time for revenge," Kane told the family.

Revenge was one thing, but planning it in a way that the family was protected wasn't going to be easy. Our parents, though they wanted to get involved, I wanted to make sure they were protected the most, and my husband agreed. Kane and I would take the major risks, Jeff would work his activism through social media, while Cynthia wanted to live up her Assata Shakur fantasy. Cynthia was a little too familiar with one of the greatest revolutionaries hardly spoken about in America. Our parents would play whatever role befitted people their age, and the goal was for everyone to emerge unscathed after this planned attack. Kane also decided that it was best for his parents to know as little as possible about our plans, in case the police, FBI, CIA, or any of those criminal organizations came back to terrorize the family under the false pretense of interrogation.

"Kane, I want you to know that you're gonna get full protection from our ancestors. We're gonna make sure of it. This is war, and we have to call on the God of war, Ogou (Ogun) to protect you from these devils. All of you will be protected by Ogou. Before we do anything, I'm going to need all of you to fly to New York to my house for a special ceremony, where we're going to honor our ancestors, and ask them for protection and guidance in this new endeavor that is necessary for us to undertake as a family. If some of you want to stand by your Christian values and don't want to participate, there's no ill will. Just remember, black people have been praying to their Christ for centuries now, and salvation has yet to come. The murders multiply, the injustices continue to pile up, and the marginalization, oppression and exploitation are endless. We have turned our backs on our own God, but as a people, we're constantly begging their Christ to make things better for us. It doesn't work like that. They themselves have proclaimed their God is a jealous God. Don't you think your God is a jealous God as well? Why should your God offer you salvation and protection when black people have turned their backs on their God? Most black people have converted to every religion, except their own natural spirituality, which is Vodou. These people learned the power of Vodou a long time ago, and saw its results during the Haitian Revolution, which is why they have done everything possible to remove it from you, and to create disdain around a religion that belongs only to those of us who have African ancestry. I want you to know that your God will protect you, but you have to embrace your own African spirituality." My father couldn't be any clearer and concise. I'm sure most of what he said probably sounded foreign to everyone in the room, except my family, and Kane who had been reading about African spirituality since we got married. "Sounds like a plan to me!" Cynthia jumped up to say with all the enthusiasm in the world. "I'm game," Jeff followed. "We're not gonna be sacrificing chickens and goats and shit, right?" Mr. Black asked. "It's not a sacrifice. Just because you don't see how the chicken or other meat that you eat every day is slaughtered, it doesn't mean they weren't killed before they were sent to your local supermarkets," my father responded. "Dad, if you're wondering if we're gonna be drinking chicken blood, or goat blood, take that out of your mind. That's white people's way of demonizing African spirituality with their Hollywood bullshit. That's not what it's about. I'm looking forward to the ceremony, Mr. Joseph. Thanks for offering to protect this family," Kane told everyone in the room.

Everyone had spoken their piece, except the two matriarchs of the family, my mother and Kane's mom. "Whatever my husband decides to do, I will support him. I don't know anything about no Haitian Vodou, but my son has been educating us about Haiti since he met his wife, and he's done a great job. I know that Haiti is the only Black Country in the world to have successfully revolted against slavery and gain its independence, while fighting the mightiest armies of France, Spain, and Great Britain. And all that happened because the Haitians relied on their African spirituality that most people refer to as Vodou, and called on their ancestors to guide them through the revolution. That much I know, and it's historical fact. I don't see why we shouldn't try a different approach. Being on our knees, begging white people for justice, while marching, hasn't gotten us anywhere. Maybe the revolution should start with a new mindset," said Mrs. Black. "It's settled then. The family will be in New York as soon as you want us there," Mr. Black announced. I was waiting for my mother to finally say something, and she did. "I'm happy to see the two families have decided to come together to fight the murder of our grandsons together. Before I met my husband, I was a Christian, just like you, and I didn't know much about African spirituality, or Vodou if you will. However, after learning so much from this man about my roots, spirituality, culture, and heritage, I embrace it fully. Vodou is not evil. No African has gone around the world using Vodou to enslave, rape, murder, or kidnap people, under the false pretense of superiority. That's what white people have done throughout the world with their Christianity. We have to recognize it's a new day, and we must acknowledge their history and who they are as a people who have manipulated their way to the top of the world by stepping on everybody through colonization. That is their history. All lessons learned come from history. We have yet to apply the lessons taught by the Haitian Revolution. It's about time. I can't wait to host the entire family in New York," my mother told the family.

It was great to see our family forming a united front to deal with the deaths of our sons, but first, we had to plan their funerals. Support poured in from everywhere. A random black person who sympathized with our loss created a Gofundme campaign to help alleviate the cost of the funeral. We didn't really need financial assistance with the funeral of our sons, because my husband and I had made the decision to purchase life insurance for our sons when they were born. The half-a-million dollar coverage on each of them was able to cover the cost of the funeral and then some. We chose to donate the money to a charity that helped fight injustice against black people by the police. We appreciated the gesture, but we knew there were more people in need of the money than we were. We didn't want to capitalize financially off the deaths of our sons. My husband and I have always been financially astute, so we always planned carefully, when it comes to our family.

THE FUNERAL

We had to wait until an autopsy was performed before we could lay our sons to rest. In the meantime, the media was trying to find any angle to place the blame on our sons for their own murders. When they couldn't find reasons like truancy, poor grades at school, juvenile delinquency, or anything negative that would support their bullshit narratives to make the cop emerge as a hero, they started attacking me and my wife's parental skills. One station called the situation "poor parenting" during a 6 o'clock news sequence, telling the audience that my wife and I were irresponsible for allowing our 11-year-old sons to leave the house with their toy guns, without giving consideration to the current climate, given the fact that there were protests all over the country for the murder of George Floyd at the hands of scumbag killer police officer, Derek Chauvin. We realized it was us against the world, and that these people had no compassion whatsoever, when it came to black people. A cop pulled out his gun to shoot two young boys without asking any questions, but the media managed to spin the blame onto the parents? What kind of world have these monsters created for black people? Every black person in America is positioned to be victimized in every way, aspect, and facet of life. We can't win against these devils. Whenever I used to think about the long list of black people who have died for no reason other than being black at the hands of police, I wondered why their family members never did anything to retaliate. And now, there I was facing the calamity that many people in the black community had been facing for years.

I needed to focus on planning the best sendoff my sons could possibly have. My sons' deaths had started to garner national attention, and a lot of black people were reaching their boiling point with the police nationwide. The mayor, police chief, and all the other public officials came out with the typical bullshit public statement about allowing the investigation process to take its course, and that justice would prevail, which was just par for the course and a publicity campaign to keep the people calm. Still, the body-cam footage had not been released by the police department. Whether it was being doctored, or they were trying to control the agitation of the people in the black community who were ready to burn down the damn city out of frustration, by holding back the footage, I had no idea. One thing I knew, though. The killer cop was not charged. He was placed on paid leave, while my family struggled with the deaths of our sons. I had to be strong for my wife, because she was overwhelmed with the fact that she had lost both of her sons to a police shooting, something we actually discussed with our sons to keep them protected. The entire time, while we were making funeral arrangements for the boys, I could tell my wife wasn't really together mentally, and the focus wasn't there. "We shouldn't have to bury our kids. They'd never broken any laws or committed any crime. Our children shouldn't have been taken away from us. It's not fair," she said to me through teary eyes, while we were sitting in the office of the funeral director. I decided to take charge of the funeral arrangements. We needed closure, but we knew that wouldn't come any time soon, based on the other cases that set the precedence for the duration for justice to be handed out to other victimized black families of police shootings. Killer cops were protected.

I had never been through the funeral or burial process before, because I never had to make arrangements for a funeral. However, the funeral director was more than accommodating, and he offered to give us a huge discount, because he was the only black-owned funeral parlor in the area. We understood and appreciated his gesture, but we saw no reason for him to discount his price, just because we were black. We opted to pay the full price he would normally charge for a funeral. At this point, I was the primary decision maker, but I also wanted my wife's opinion and support in anything that I decided. We both wanted a traditional ceremony, because of the family. However, we decided to cremate the boys, as a personal choice that my wife and I agreed on. Their ashes would be at home with us, and we wouldn't have to worry about their headstone being shot annually by scumbag racist cops, who have shot Fred Hampton's headstone, the young leader of the Black Panther Party in Chicago, in case the killer cop is found guilty. There was no reason to purchase a burial plot because my wife and I never intended on having our bodies buried anywhere. We chose to have an open casket visitation, in order to keep the boys' memory alive in everyone's mind for as long as possible, so no one would forget about our fight for justice. We chose a beautiful urn that would sit on our mantle at home, until we're called home ourselves. It was also important to us that our sons' funeral didn't turn into a charade for the likes of reverend Al Sharpton. We weren't looking for that type of attention. Still, the media wouldn't leave us alone. We allowed limited media coverage to keep the shooting of our sons fresh in people's minds on the news, but we didn't hire an attorney right away. There was no statement made publicly by me or my wife about the killing. We left them wondering what our next move would be.

We tried our best to pick the most beautiful caskets for our sons, their suits, and the other necessities for the funeral. When the pastor asked how many people we were expecting to attend the funeral, we really couldn't give him a definitive answer, because we wanted some members of the public to have limited access to the funeral as well. As many black people as possible needed to see how black children were being gunned down by these race soldiers who are hired and trained to protect and serve our community. I wasn't going to part with the innocence of my boys so quickly. I wanted the world to see their youthful, nonthreatening faces, so they would know why they didn't deserve to die. I wanted every black parent to feel our loss, our pain, so they could be galvanized and joined us in our fight to get justice for our sons.

My brother decided to write the most beautiful poem dedicated to our sons, which was included in the obituary. We had taken a beautiful picture of our boys while we were on a family trip to Virginia, and it was the perfect picture for the obituary. We gave the funeral director all the necessary information he needed to start the process, such as our boys' birth certificates, social security numbers, and their life insurance information, to pay for the funeral. The date of service was set for two weeks on the second Saturday after their murder, which gave our extended family time to make travel arrangements. Most of our family members were coming from New York City and Boston.

As expected, the funeral went on without a hitch. My sister read her own poem she had written for our boys, which brought the house to tears. A few of the boys' friends and teachers had nothing but kind words to say on their behalf. Our sons were very respectful, always courteous and cordial to others, and great students at school. The family decided to celebrate their lives at the repast at my house. However, while at the house, my cousin Trey approached me and said, "I know you're not just gonna take this shit sitting down, right, cuz?" Trey wasn't one to accept bullshit and defeat from anybody. We had grown up together in Boston, and Trey feared nothing and no one. Trey wasn't the type of dude to let anything go. He was a couple of years older than me, but was also my protector in the streets when we were young. Any beef that I had with anybody anywhere, Trey was always the person I called to help me settle any threat. "You know I can't, Trey. I have to do something," I told him. "Well, I'm here at your service. You know I hate flying, so I drove down from Boston, and you know I ride dirty all the time. Just let me know when you're ready to take care of that pig," he said. While I really wanted to address the situation with Trey right then and there, I had the responsibility of making sure the family was enjoying themselves. "We'll talk once everyone leaves. I know you always have my back, cuz," I told him. "For sho," he responded in his street slang. Before I forgot, I needed to know where Trey was staying while he was in Georgia. "By the way, you've got somewhere to stay while you're down here?" I asked. He smiled at me and said, "You know I've had them in every area code way before Luda was rapping about it. You know how I do." Trey wasn't lying. He was one of those pretty boy street dudes that people underestimated because of his looks. He always had a way with the ladies, and he could hold his own in the streets. "I see you, player," I said to him, before walking back to the main family room, which was open to the kitchen and dining room, where most of my family gathered. It felt kind of good to see Trey, because it gave me the reassurance that I wasn't in this thing alone.

My family was no different than any other normal black family. We could go on for years without talking to one another, but when it's time for the family to come together, we always find each other. I hadn't talked to Trey in a while, but I always knew what was going on with him, because my mom kept me updated on his life. Trey was not exactly who I would call a role model in the family, but he was loved and respected by everyone in the family, because of his love for his family. He had a couple of baby mamas, and the typical drama that most street guys deal with, but Trey was all about family. He was always smart enough to avoid prison, but he stayed in the streets. He couldn't leave the street life alone. While a lot of people in the family didn't agree with his street lifestyle, many of them would call on Trey whenever there was a threat against them. Trey protected the reputation of the family. He was always ride or die for the family, especially, my mom, because she was his favorite aunt. My mother was the only person who never judged Trey as a person. She accepts who he is, and loves him just as much as she loves her own children. Trey used to love coming to the house when we were younger. Trey had all types of street connections all the way up and down the east coast. He only showed up to family events when his presence was necessary. He didn't want to burden anyone with his lifestyle, or jeopardize the lives of those of us who didn't live that life. It was his own way of showing respect to the family, but he was always available whenever he was called upon. I was very happy to see Trey.

After everyone left the house, I decided to have a one-on-one with Trey, so that we could execute a plan for revenge. However, Trey had a surprise for me when he showed up with one of my wife's cousins from New York. "This is my man, Big J.P. He's your wife's cousin from Brooklyn," he introduced us formally. I hadn't had a chance to meet all the members of my wife's family formally, but I met Big J.P in passing, and he apparently had more in common with Trey, and they decided to form an alliance to help me seek the justice that I knew would never come from the District Attorney's office. I could see why people called him Big J.P, because he was huge. He stood about 6 ft 5 inches tall and weighed over 350 lbs easy, but he seemed nimble on his feet. He wasn't sloppy or burly big, but more athletically big. "Big J.P is family. We can discuss whatever plan you want with him around," Trey told me. Trey had his way of identifying true loyal street soldiers, and he vouched for Big J.P. My wife had never really talked about her distant family members that much, but I was shocked to see so many of her family members from New York at the funeral. Street people seem to think along the same line, because Big J.P had also driven down from New York, and he was riding just as dirty as Trey.

After discussing the plan with the fellas, we felt it was best that Trey and Big J.P to lay low, because everything was still fresh, and we didn't want a magnifying glass on us. Trey decided to leave his arsenal in Atlanta for safekeeping and promised to return once we got word whether the killer cop was going to be indicted or not. He never divulged to me where he had left his stash of weapons. I'm sure he and Big J.P collaborated on a hiding place, but I didn't want to know. From my personal assessment, Big J.P seemed like a solid, trustworthy guy who believed in street ethics like Trey, and was more than willing to be part of the brigade seeking justice for my sons' deaths. I grew more confident with the support cast, because I felt like had a couple of ride or dies with me, and they would make sure we'd see things through, if it ever came to that.

Once the celebration of my sons' lives ended, most of our family members went back to their respective homes and states the following day. There were some long goodbyes and there were short ones, but the entire family came together in grief. Black folks always unite at weddings and funerals. We're gonna have to do better than that. Our parents stayed a few days longer to comfort us, but my two siblings had to return home for work. I was happy that so many family members flew down to Atlanta to support me and my wife. It turned out to be a celebration of family. My wife's family got better acquainted with my family in the process because a lot of them didn't make it to Haiti for our wedding.

LIFE GOES ON?

Unfortunately for me and my husband, life couldn't just go on. There were too many reminders around the house, and the deafening silence was unbearable at times, because we were used to our boys making a decent amount of noise as normal children would. Everything in our house reminded us of our boys, even the very reason why we moved to Gwinnett County. We thought we were doing something great for our children and family when we decided to purchase a home in the suburb, to provide a safer environment for them. We were no different than many other high-achieving black families who thought relocating to the suburbs from the "destructive environment" in the hood would prolong the lives of our children, and provide relief from the chaos they might've had to face while growing up there. My husband and I, both, grew up in the inner city, and we managed with no problem. For some reason, we had fallen victim to a mentality and practice that most professional black people have been indoctrinated into. We started to lose ourselves because of our accomplishments, and began to believe the very people we grew up around had become too dangerous for us to live among them, and our children would fare better around people less familiar with their culture, and who didn't look like them. It's the most backward way of thinking, but a lot of black people have fallen victim to that propaganda. We paid the highest and dear price to learn that lesson. My husband and I felt the death of our children was a sacrifice for the move to the suburbs. Though our community was a mixture of folks, still, I wouldn't call it a melting pot. I had heard the horror stories from some of our black neighbors who had integrated the area earlier than we did. Their white neighbors made it hell for them when they first moved in, by calling them names, cutting their eyes at them, spray painting their cars and home with derogatory racial slurs, when all they wanted was a safe place for their children. They fought through the racism, humiliation, and everything else they had to face in the suburbs, and subjected their children to black token status in their white schools, without realizing they could have easily used the same effort and energy to change for the better, the black communities they were running from.

Sometimes I feel that black people hate each other more than the racists who have taught some of us to hate ourselves. After my sons died, I felt like a traitor. I shouldn't have ever abandoned my own community to move to another community where I had to force acceptance on a group of people who hate me for absolutely no reason other than the color of my skin. Few black people take the time to analyze the origin and root of our hatred for each other. We didn't come into this world with hearts filled with hate. How did that come about? The deaths of my sons forced me into a critical thinking and research mode. I started reading all types of books on the psychology of black people, as well as the psychology of hatred and its impact, on not just black people, but the world. Through my research, I came to the conclusion that hatred is something that white people established in the world long ago for dominance, but more specifically, their hatred for black people, was borne out of fear and insecurities, in order to control people, labor, and resources that didn't belong to them across Africa.

Life couldn't just go on for me and my husband, because our children had become the center of our lives for the past 11 years. We had dedicated our every effort and love to their development, at least until they were to become self-sufficient, productive adults who would make us proud. All of that was taken from us in a blink of an eye, and this society made us feel powerless, as if we couldn't do anything about the murder of our sons at the hands of a cop. I had to think long and hard about the proposition that I was presented with by my cousin, Big J.P. He had become the enforcer of the family, something most of the family members frowned upon, unless they needed Big J.P to do something illegal for them. He had grown to become the quintessential "thug" that most of our family members fearfully whispered about. He was born and raised in the Bedford Stuyvesant section of Brooklyn. Most of my cousin's friends were drug dealers and street thugs, so he did everything in his power to fit in, and not show fear of his peers. When he was growing up in Brooklyn, being Haitian meant his friends had their own prejudices about his Haitian culture, and they didn't always accept him as just another one of their black friends. Some of them even gave him the nickname Haitian J. P. They were always making fun of him when he was younger because his parents didn't waste their money dressing him in the latest designer name-brand clothing and shoes, so he always had to defend himself, and got into a lot of fights as a result. The older he got, the more street he became, and the tougher outer layer he developed, in order to survive the streets of Brooklyn. He became what everyone in the family feared the most, a (ti thug), a Haitian definition of a tyrant thug, and a bully to anybody who dared disrespect his Haitian culture in his presence. Big J.P was very sensitive about his Haitian heritage. In addition, my cousin's huge intimidating size instilled fear in almost everyone who met him. He grew over 6ft tall when he was still in middle school. He had an interest in sports and played football for a short while, but that interest waned when he started hanging out with the wrong crowd. The dominance of Hip Hop culture in his environment influenced the way Big J.P talked, the way he walked, the way he dressed, and his overall decorum, especially in Haitian settings. He was the prototypical outcast in the Haitian community. Talk about an identity crisis, he went through it all. His family thought he acted too African-American, and his African-American peers made fun of him because he was Haitian. Nonetheless, my cousin was a big teddy bear, but when pushed, he could turn into a killer Grizzly bear. I was one of a few people who understood him, and it is for that reason that we grew closer.

Big J.P and I bonded for the first time when my parents took me to a party at one of my dad's distant cousins' house in Elmont, Long Island. We were just 7 years old at the time and didn't understand what the hell the grown-ups were doing at the party. It was a typical Haitian first communion celebration for one of our other cousins. Old Haitian Kompa music was on blast on the speakers, for most of the night, and the DJ would only play something that we could relate to as children, like Hip Hop or R&B, after bugging him to death. Haiti's famous Barbancourt rum and Prestige beer was flowing all night among the adults, which is customary at these Haitian parties.There was ample food sitting on the table to be served later to the people at the party; from macaroni au gratin, as my Haitian family called macaroni and cheese, diri ak djon djon (black rice), griyo (fried pork), tasso (fried goat), gravy and a few other kinds of meats and rice, which was enough to feed a village. Most Haitians usually throw a big feast to celebrate their children's first communion, the irony of the Catholic religion that is lost on most Haitians who call themselves proud of their African heritage, but hey! My dad never missed a family party when I was little. He always took us to every party and every celebration that our extended family or his close friends invited him to. It was his way of keeping himself and his family connected to the rest of the family and his community.

Most Haitian immigrants usually bear the financial brunt of newly arrived family members from Haiti, and my mom and dad were no different. We had tons of family members who moved to the States from Haiti, and my parents always had an open door policy for them, because of the struggles they went through when they first got here. Big J.P's mom was my dad's first cousin, but they acted more like sisters and brothers with one another. She stayed with us for a couple of years until she was able to get her own place after she met Big J.P's dad. After my family moved from Brooklyn, we didn't see the extended family much. It was always at the occasional parties that the family would catch up. Through the years, Big J.P and I kept in touch. He had even talked about moving to Atlanta at one point, to get away from the hustle and bustle of New York. However, these street guys never know when to quit hustling. Every time I talked to Big J.P, he told me the same thing, "His next deal would be his last." His last deal never came, and I just kept my fingers crossed that he didn't end up in federal prison; or worse yet, dead. I was happy to see him show up for the funeral. I never approved of Big J.P's street hustling, but he became a product of his environment. Unfortunately, a lot of immigrants from Haiti tend to believe there's a distinction between public and private schools because that's how it is in Haiti. There's a certain level of of respect associated with private schools and the children who attend them in Haiti, while kids who attend public schools are looked down upon. However, in America, children who live in the hood and attend private schools are ridiculed and seen as soft. Big J.P fell victim to that social ill in the hood. Big J.P always had to prove himself, because his friends thought he was soft, and would often call him "private school boy." His parents' decision to send him to private school while still living in the hood was a recipe for disaster.

Before he became known to the streets as Big J.P, the family affectionately called him Jean Paul. My aunt and her husband worked two jobs each, so they could make sure my cousin had the best education. However, in the process, they also ended up neglecting Jean Paul. The only parental supervision my cousin ever received was from his non-English speaking grandmother that his parents left in the house with him every day, while they spent 16 hours at their jobs, busting their asses to help pay for his private school, put food on the table, a roof over his head, and to send money back home to extended family they left behind in Haiti. My cousin was actually the prototypical Haitian child who was in the house with an elder who had no idea what he was talking about with his friends. The language barrier gave Big J.P free rein to do whatever he wanted to do, and to plan his escape from the house whenever his grandmother fell asleep. He was the apple of her eye, as the only grandchild she ever had, so she was a little lenient whenever she discovered he snuck out the house. She would keep it from his dad, because his dad would whip him like a slave. She hated seeing my cousin beaten to a pulp by his father. As much as his grandmother cautioned him about the streets, Big J.P couldn't stay away. Drug has always been a problem in the black community, coupled with other crimes that have swallowed plenty of our family members, but Big J.P thought he had it under control, just like the other millions of drug dealers who came before him. The fast money, fast cars, women, and jewelry were all part of the tunnel vision. Prison, getting shot, and being murdered prematurely are never part of the foresight. Still, Big J.P was a sweet boy who grew up to be a man that nobody wanted to cross. I'm just lucky that he's my cousin, and he's on my side.

Apparently, Big J.P and Trey were pretty fond of each other, and they decided to work together on their own revenge plans while protecting my husband and me. I didn't ask what their plans were, but they assured me that we would get revenge for our boys. I wanted assurance that they weren't both going to end up in jail, but the response I got from both of them was not what I expected, "Jail is the risk that comes with the territory. Sometimes you gotta do what you gotta do," Big J.P told me, while Trey shook his head in agreement. It was bad enough that we lost two sons, but I certainly didn't want us to lose two cousins in the process.

BACK TO LIFE

After burying our children, my wife and I struggled to return to our normal lives. I was able to take a few days off from work, as did my wife, to grieve the death of our sons a while longer, but we knew that the bereavement period wasn't coming to an end any time soon. You don't just move on after the children you brought into this world are killed. Still, we needed to get ready to deal with the legal ramifications of the case. We discussed our plans moving forward, regarding legal representation and what we would do to memorialize our boys. There were plenty of attorneys knocking on our door to represent us, because the county stood no litigating chance in a civil lawsuit in court. However, we decided to hire the most reputable black law firm in Atlanta, and we made sure they would be able to honor our request not to turn the deaths of our sons into a spectacle or publicity stunt for their firm. We didn't want to create another Ben Crump. We wanted to quietly settle this case, and allow the other pieces attached to the case to fall where they may. We were not foolish enough to allow these people to get away with the murder of our sons in all aspects. We wanted something out of it, and we wanted the entire black community to benefit and be better, at the expense of the death of our sons. That's the least we could do. We weren't too concerned about the amount of money we could get from the county. We were more interested in making sure this never happened again to another black family, and we wanted to establish a legacy to keep the memories of our innocent sons alive for as long as we could. My wife came up with the idea of creating a scholarship fund in their names with the settlement money that we might receive from the county. We didn't want a cent of that blood money to be any part of our lifestyle. We'd planned on giving away every cent. That's not what ended up happening.

It was while watching our local news a few days after we buried our sons that we learned a grand jury had decided not to prosecute the killer cop who murdered our sons. I wasn't just baffled by the lack of action against this cop, but the audacity of these white people to decide not to prosecute a cop who murdered two innocent boys behooved me to heed the warning of white supremacy in this country. I knew things would get worse before they got better. It was time to spring into action. This killer cop was able to keep his job and have the opportunity to murder somebody else's child? Not on my watch! I had promised my wife we were going to get justice for our boys, and I intended to do just that. One of my heroes was Christopher Dorner, a former officer with the Los Angeles police department, who decided to take revenge against the LAPD in Orange County, Los Angeles County, Riverside County, and San Bernardino County in California. He was able to terrorize them for 9 days before they were able to locate and kill him. I had already come to the conclusion that I was a dead man walking, but I damn sure didn't plan on dying by myself. This is not something that I could reveal to my wife. I knew she'd be okay after we received the settlement, but as a precautionary measure, I created a trust with all of our assets, just to protect her from all the things that I had planned on doing to these cops. This was going to be terror they never anticipated. Dorner had left behind a manifesto, which I read, but more importantly, he left behind a blueprint to execute my plans much better than he ever did.

My wife and I were regulars at the shooting range in Stone Mountain. We had always been gun enthusiasts. All of the guns that we had were legally purchased and registered with the state. If I used any of these guns, I might as well have walked into a police station to turn myself in, because they would trace the ballistics back to me so fast, I wouldn't have anywhere to hide. I needed to make sure that any gun that I used couldn't directly be traced back to me. I told my cousin Trey to get me a sniper rifle and a semi-automatic rifle, an AK-47, an AR-15 with silencers, and plenty of ammo. He assured me one of his people who owned a mechanic shop in New York could produce the silencers. While I was happy that Trey and

Big J.P offered their help, it was my job to personally avenge the deaths of my sons.

Life as we knew it would not even be worth living anymore, if I didn't avenge the deaths of my sons. I needed the satisfaction of justice, and I had planned on getting it, even if I had to become a lone vigilante. Not long after it was announced on the news that the cop would not be charged, my phone rang. It was my cousin Trey asking me to get ready, because he was on his way. We didn't speak so clearly that my wife could understand, but we understood each other's coded words. He'd also mentioned that Big J.P was coming down with him, and to keep it a secret from my wife. My wife was a total wreck, because she was sitting next to me when the DA announced there would be no charges against the cop during a press release on television. She balled up and ran to the bedroom, while I sat on the couch pondering my next move. My wife was always the voice of reason in the family, so I didn't know if it was okay to let her in on my plans. I decided against telling her what I had planned to do. First things first, I needed to make sure that Trey was able to get all the weapons, ammo, and silencers that I asked him to get me. To my surprise, Trey told me that everything I needed was already in his bag of arsenal that he brought down when he came to the funeral. The only thing missing was the Sniper rifle, which he planned on bringing down with him, with enough ammo to blow up a city. He didn't even bother asking me to send him any money, because he knew I was good for it, and didn't want any large amount of money transferred to him to be traced by the FBI or any other law enforcement agency.

Before I could rationalize my thoughts for my next plan of action, my brother, Jeff, called to let me know that he had already mobilized thousands of his followers on social media for a march scheduled in front of the police headquarters in Gwinnett County the next day. My brother had always been a low-key social activist, but the death of my sons pushed him right to the forefront of activism. He was a full-blown activist who was ready to take center stage at the rally he organized. He wasn't going to wait on BLM to take action. This was personal. I was actually proud of my brother. I don't know how he and my sister were able to book their flights so quickly, but they called and told us they were coming to stir shit up in Atlanta, and to be ready. I was game! My wife was game! My entire family was game! And so were my in-laws!

THE PROCESS

It didn't take long for our lawyer to call us to explain the procedural steps for the lawsuit he filed on our behalf. I know I said we didn't want a dime of their money, but it doesn't mean the black community couldn't use that money, and we wanted to make damn sure of it. He had met with Gwinnett County's lawyers, and an offer was made to settle the case. They wanted to expedite the settlement a lot quicker than usual, because they didn't want Gwinnett County to be known as the racist haven that it is, especially after a racist grand jury decided not to indict the killer cop. The amount of money offered to us would've been difficult for most families to pass up, but my wife and I had already made the decision we didn't want a cent of that money for personal use, so we ended up playing hardball to get even more money. If we could've bankrupted the entire county, that's what we would have done. We sent our lawyers back to the drawing board to get us as much money as they possibly knew existed in the coffers of Gwinnett County. If these people were so eager to settle, they understood their officer was in the wrong. Still, they didn't fire him for violating department procedure. We wanted to make sure the scholarship fund in the names of our sons would be funded for a long time to come.

Meanwhile, my brother, Jeff, and my sister, Cynthia, had landed in Atlanta, picked up their rental car from the airport, and drove straight down to the office of a local activist to go over their plans for the gathering at police headquarters in Snellville. They only called to let us know they were in Atlanta, so we could participate in the march, if we wanted to, but we didn't have to. My wife and I opted not to go on the first day. It would've been too emotional for her. Also, I wanted to get a feel of the atmosphere before we got involved. All the local news media were on site covering the march. While a local reporter interviewed my brother, Jeff, he made it clear that they were demanding that police release the body-cam footage, because this was the only proof that was needed to show that this cop had acted precariously and in a negligent manner, as it relates to his duties as a law upholding police officer. Jeff didn't exactly want to reveal who he was to the reporter who kept pressing him about his identity. "Can you tell us what your relationship is to the movement and the victim in this case? Are you a Georgia resident?" She kept coming at him with all types of questions, but Jeff was a professional. He had been training for this moment. "What difference does it make who I am? You should care more about the reasons why all these black people have to keep gathering all across the country ever so often for the same reason, to demand justice for black murder victims at the hands of police. We are here seeking justice for something that is too prevalent between black people and the police, because these police departments refuse to properly train their police officers to remove their biases, and hold them accountable when they violate the rights of citizens, especially when they take the lives of black children and black people," Jeff responded. "Well, what can I say to that? You have a point. Good luck in your efforts to seek justice for these two young men," the reporter told my brother, with some compassion in her voice, because as a black woman, she felt his pain and sincerity to seek justice for the boys. The camera was quickly cut off, as the station went to a commercial. I guess she had gone off script, and compassion on the part of a black reporter was off-limits.

I saw plenty of people on television at the march wearing t-shirts with my sons' pictures with the printed texts, "Justice for the twins." My sister, Cynthia, was the one in charge of making sure that everyone carried a sign with the symbols of injustice against black people nationwide. All the names of the past victims of police brutality across the country were written on different signs carried by different people throughout the crowd. Through my own research into police brutality against black people, I learned that since the murder of George Floyd in Minneapolis, MN, 229 black people have fallen victim to police killings. These people's deaths were not sensationalized like some of the other well-known victims of police brutality, but I decided to write down a few names for my own anecdotes: Tony McDade, 38, Tallahassee, FL, Modesto Reyes, 35 Marrero, LA, Ruben Smith III, 35, North Little Rock, AK, Jarvis Sullivan Yulee, 44, FL, Terrell Mitchell, 34, Philadelphia, PA, Momodou Lamin Sisay, 34, Snellville, GA, Derrick Thompson, 46, Fountain, FL, David McAtee, 53, Louisville, KY, Tyquarn Graves, 33, Brooklyn, NY, Kamal Flowers, 24, New Rochelle, NY, Lewis Ruffin Jr., 38, Orlando, FL, Phillip Jackson, 32, Tunnel Hill, GA, Michael Blu Thomas, 63, Lancaster, CA, Rayshard Brooks, 27, Atlanta, GA, Cane Van Pelt, 23, Crown Point, IN, Donald Ward, 27, Phoenix, AZ, Brandon Gardner, 24, Beach Park, IL, Terron Jammal Boone, 31, Rosamond, CA, Derrick Canada, 43, in Giddings, TX, Skyleur Toung, 31, San Bernardino, CA, Robert D'Lon Harris, Vinita, OK, Rasheed Mathew Moorman, 26, Roanoke, VA, Aloysius Larue Keaton, 58, Little Rock, AK, Ken O'Ruffin, 32, Sheboygan, WI, KY Johnson, 31 Kansas City, MO, William Wade Burgess III, 27, St. Louis, MO, Joseph Denton, 35, Milwaukee, WI, Paul Williams, Houston, TX, Malik Canty 36, Paterson, NJ, Erroll Johnson, 31 Monroe, LA, Richard Lewis Price, 49, San Diego, CA, Hakim Littleton, 20, Detroit Michigan, Vincent Demario Truit, 17, Austell, GA, Aaron Anthony Hudson, 31, Syracuse, NY, Darius Washington, 24, Chicago, IL, Vincent Harris, 51, Baton Rouge, LA, Jeremy Southern, 22, Sacramento, CA, Chester Jenkins, 60, Stockton, CA, David Earl Brooks, Jr., 45, Roxboro, NC, Darrien Walker, 28, Detroit, MI, Ashton Broussard, 30,

Houston, TX, Amir Johnson, 30 Ventnor City, NJ, Julian Edward Roosevelt Lewis, 60, Sylvania, GA, Salaythis Melvin, 22, Orlando, FL, Jonathan Jefferson, Bossier City, LA, Rafael Jevon Minniefield, 29, Moreland, GA, Kendrell Antron Watkins, 31, Tuscaloosa, AL, Anthony McClain, 32, Pasadena, CA, Adrian Jason Roberts, 37, Hope Mills, NC, Trayford Pellerin, 31, Lafayette, LA, and the list goes on and on. I truly feel terrible that I didn't even have the patience to write down the names of all the 229 victims, because the list was so long. The killings spread across the entire country, from every corner without prejudice limited to age and gender. However, I found it interesting that the majority of police killings take place in California and Louisiana. Though Georgia was more of a midlevel exception on the list, I learned that my sons weren't the first people to be murdered by Snellville Police. 39-year-old Momodou Lamin Sisay, son of a retired Gambian United Nations employee was fatally shot in Snellville, GA on May 29th, 2020. There hasn't been too much dialogue about his death in the media. I didn't want my sons' deaths to become anecdotal. I needed to solidify the guilt of this police officer, without leaving any room for doubt. I had to prove his motive was racist, and that his destructive behavior against black people was habitual.

THE FAMILY TEAM

We went through so much agony and pain, this fight was no longer about our boys anymore. My sons' deaths had finally become national news, almost a year after the death of George Floyd, although they were murdered a couple of months after the death of George Floyd in Minneapolis. The media spotlight was now shifted to my family, whether we wanted it or not. My wife and I have always been private people, so we decided to delegate the media duties to my brother Jeff and my sister Cynthia. They were going to be our mouthpiece in the media, because we knew they could handle it. Everybody had a role to play in our plans to get revenge for my sons, but a couple of people decided to just lurk in the shadows, to keep from agitating my wife and other family members. However, I was always aware of their involvement in the plan. My wife had decided it wouldn't have been a good idea if my cousin Trey and her cousin Big J.P got involved. I agreed with her on principles, but Trey and Big J.P were already in too deep to back out. I didn't want them to pull out of the plan that we had set forth to make revenge an attainable goal. They were already in

Georgia doing the leg work to make sure this cop never killed again. They had become my silent/ghost associates. My wife didn't have a clue what was going on. I wanted to keep it that way to protect her. There were too many risks involved, and I didn't want my wife to constantly worry about another family member.

Since I have a background in computer science, and after working in that field for so many years to serve other people, I figured I might as well use my skills to serve me for once. I decided to dig deep into the background of Officer Kevin McNeal, the officer who shot my sons, and wouldn't you know it? I found some of his old posts expressing his racist vitriol toward black people. Of course, I handed copies of his social media rants from Facebook, Instagram, and Twitter to my attorney, so he could build a stronger case for the civil lawsuit, because I was certain that the prosecutor was already aware of his racist past. Still, when my lawyer decided to bring his history of racist ideologies toward black people to the prosecutor, he dismissed them as the growing pains of a 21-year-old. At least, that's what my attorney told me. This racist shot my young sons who were constantly being referred to as men by the media, because they were above average height and weight for their age, but somehow there wasn't a shortage of compassion available to identify a grown ass man as a racist? My blood was boiling by this point, and I knew something had to be done. I decided to embark on my own campaign to destroy the expose the true character of Officer Kevin McNeal. I created social media pages on Twitter and Instagram called "The Twins' Deaths." Every day I woke up, I started posting about my boys, while reposting all the old racist posts from Officer McNeal that the police department tried to bury, in order to make their police department look nonracist. In no time, the social media accounts gained a few hundred thousand followers, and words were spreading that fast that Officer McNeal had a racist history prior to joining the police department, and he was still posting racist content after becoming a police officer.

Meanwhile, Jeff and Cynthia woke up every day and drove to police headquarters in Snellville with their crew, to make sure the case stayed relevant in the media. They kept up the pressure on the police chief to fire Officer McNeal, but the police chief claimed his hands were tied because the killer officer wasn't charged with the deaths of my sons. The whole thing had become a charade, and I knew we were never going to get any justice for my sons. I made a request to my lawyer to speed up the negotiating process for the settlement, because I knew I was going to need the money for a few reasons, but none personal. My brother and sister had decided they were going to be in this fight for the long haul, so they decided to extend their stay in Atlanta to keep pressure on the police department, while Trey and Big J.P were more in the trenches that circumvent the entire situation. They were watching the killer cop, the prosecutor, the medical examiner who determined the case wasn't a homicide, and everyone else who played a role in making sure the killer cop was absolved of culpability in the deaths of my sons. What baffled me the most was the fact that the medical examiner determined that my sons' deaths were not considered homicides. How he came to that conclusion? I have no idea.

I wasn't looking for sympathy from the public, I just wanted to expose the killer cop for the racist that he is. The longer I dug into his past, the more incidents that popped up. He had more than 6 encounters with black people in the past who filed complaints against him, because he used a racial epithet to malign them, and excessive force while placing them under arrest without just cause. There was definitely a history that the police department chose to ignore. However, what was the most alarming was the fact that over 95% of this racist piece of shit's arrests consisted of black people, in a city where black folks make up only 39% of the population. Despite the fact of this history being presented to the prosecutor, he still opted to use a favorable grand jury comprised of primarily white people, to ensure this officer wasn't indicted. After the deaths of my sons, I realized there were multiple components to the level of racism black people have faced in the justice department. Judges, prosecutors, cops, medical examiners, and even grand juries, all work in cahoots, when it comes to protecting white supremacy and racism in this country. To dismantle such a system, it would take just as many years as it took to abolish slavery legally, but not necessarily officially. As it relates to slavery, most people have no idea that the 13th Amendment still needs to be ratified to remove slavery completely from the constitution. During my quest for justice for my sons, I discovered that President Obama spent 8 years in the white house, and never took the time to address the fact that the US Constitution has an exclusion clause that still makes it legal for people to be enslaved while incarcerated. Where's all the "hope and change" that President Obama was bringing to the people during his 8 years as president? That's the platform this former Harvard-educated black attorney used to get elected, but he failed the very people who believed in his ideology of hope and change. He was just another puppet out for self, and a tool used to further marginalize black people.

The more I researched the history of injustice against black people in this country, the more monumental the fight for justice appeared to be. No amount of evidence is enough to convince white people that racism is the underlying factor for injustice against black people in this country. The absurdity of the legal system in this country is basically a jab at human rights and democracy everywhere. These pretenders in America have set up their own guidelines to mask the corruption they've created around the world, in order to control people and resources, and it all stems from racism. The mechanisms set in place for America to corrupt the rest of the world, while proclaiming itself the god of morality and democracy are ludicrous. Much like a pyramid scheme where people are bamboozled into believing better returns are guaranteed for their investments, the American government sits at the helm of a corrupted pyramid, as it expands and dictates corruption in every region of the world. If a country or leader can't beat them, it's best to join them, or else they'll face sanctions, embargoes, economic destabilization, or even worse, death at the hands of the well-trained US government assassins known as the CIA, should a leader disobeys any order from the corruption king of the world.

The US has never practiced all the bullshit they've tried to force upon the world. Their police and justice departments have violated the rights of more black people here on an annual basis than in the entire rest of the world combined. They've imprisoned more black people here than in any other country on earth, without just cause. The insurmountable issues that black people have faced in this country are enough for the UN, as an international organization of peace, security, and the protection of human rights, to have intervened long ago, but they fall under the control of the corrupt US government as well. Based on the long history of injustice against black people in this country since slavery, I'm starting to believe that black people are not supposed to live among white people. As a matter of fact, black people never desired to live among white people. It was white people who embarked on their cruelty tours around the world and started to illegally kidnap, rape, murder and enslave black people against their will. Black people have populated the West because the European rejects and degenerates who left England, France, Spain, Portugal, the Netherlands, and Belgium were too lazy to work, in order to build their own wealth, in addition to having no respect for humankind. I didn't know if I wanted to deal with all that anymore. I was at my wit's end, and I was ready to go out in a blaze of glory.

While thinking of my next plan of action, I received a call from my father-in-law. He said he had something to discuss with me, but wanted to make sure that I was comfortable first, before bringing up the topic. Given the fact that I grew up in an evangelical society where my natural customs were taken away from me, and I was forced to adhere to the customs of the enslavers, my father-in-law always made it a point to preface everything by mentioning our cultural differences. He was a proud African who happened to be born in Haiti. He instilled that in his daughter and tried to cement the fact that my identity was that of white people, because they've forced their customs on everyone since they illegally stole America from the Natives, and forced Africans to live under duress during slavery for so long. "Kane, you're married to my daughter now. So you understand that you are not just my son-in-law, I consider you my son, right?" he said through the phone. I confirmed by nodding my head and saying yes on the phone. "Well, as my son, I have to teach you about your African roots, because most African-Americans are detached from their roots, because you have lived with white people for so long. The only thing left that is black or African about you are your features and your skin color. You speak their language, you're educated at their school, you eat their unhealthy foods, you adopt their customs, you celebrate their holidays, you practice their religion, you wear their clothing, and you try your best to live up to a standard they forced upon you. In essence, you are white with black skin. They basically treat you like an adopted child who has never had contact with his biological parents but yearn to reconnect with his roots. They even make you feel like you're adopted by how they treat you in their society." I had to think about what my father in law just said to me, because it went deeper than just the surface solutions that most of us seek to a complicated issue that is multi-layered. "I never thought about it that way," I responded. "Of course not, this is a multi-genera-tional problem. Your great-great-grandparents were enslaved, and all the customs forced upon them were passed down for many gen-erations to their great-grandchildren, their grandchildren, and all the way down to you. Everything that you do now seems normal to you. The consciousness of black folks in America is dormant. Black people must be awakened and reconnect with their true heritage and roots," he told me. I didn't really have any idea where the con-versation was leading other than his usual historical diatribes. "Mr. Joseph, I don't mean to cut you off, but I'm trying to figure out a way to get justice for my two sons, because my wife has been devas-tated since their deaths," I told him. He paused to listen to me for a quick second, and then said, "This is the reason why I'm calling you. You're never gonna get justice for the deaths of my grandsons, if you're waiting on the white justice system in America. However, there's always another way," he said. "What's the other way?" I asked. "I know you're an ex-military guy, and you're thinking about revenge in the physical sense with a gun, and you're gonna risk your freedom and your life. I don't wanna see my daughter lose her husband after losing her two sons. I may be Haitian, but I'm very close to my African roots. We're gonna get justice the African way, the same way my people got their independence from the white man in Haiti. We're going to invoke the spirits of our ancestors in a ritual, and you'll get the results that you seek. I just need you to believe in what I'm about to do, and everything will work out. It's all about faith, just like the faith most black people put into the white man's Christian religion that has yielded them no results, since the their enslavement. I just need you to believe and have faith," he said. At that point, I was willing to try anything, including some tribal African rituals, to get justice for my boys.

I was excited and weary at the same time, after speaking to my father-in-law. I wanted to jump on the bed next to my wife and sleep my problems away, but I couldn't. I walked into the room to find my wife looking refreshed and more upbeat than she was earlier. "You seem like you're feeling much better," I said to her. She looked at me and smiled. "Did my father call you?" she asked.

"Yeah, I spoke with your dad," I replied. "Did he tell you his plans to get us justice?" she said with much more confidence than I had ever seen since the boys were murdered. "Yes, we talked about connecting to our African roots and doing a ritual to get justice for our sons, but I'm not sure if I believe 100% that can happen," I said to her. My wife looked me dead in my eyes and said, "There are many things about my culture that you haven't learned, and I was hoping to one day discuss what I know, not you've heard, about the Vodou spirituality, with you. All that taboo bullshit from Hollywood, it's just to scare black people from their own ancestral power. They demonize Vodou to weaken black people as a group. Haiti is the only nation that successfully fought for its independence against white people, and there's a reason for that. However, Haitians lost their way and turned catholic after they were handed victory during the Haitian Revolution. You know my father is a Vodou practitioner, and my grandparents are as well. They've never done any harm to anybody. However, they can call on the spirits for protection, prosperity, and everything else, just like these people do with their white Jesus," she said to me. I didn't really know what to say, because my wife and I had never discussed her family's deep religious roots in depth like that. However, the deaths of my sons brought the entire family closer together. "Babe, I'm game for whatever you think is going to work for us to be at peace with the deaths of our sons. If you believe it can work, I believe it'll work," I told her without a doubt. "Baby, it will. Just have faith. I don't need you, my cousin,

202

or your cousin to go out there and risk your life by doing something stupid. I couldn't bear to lose another member of my family. We're gonna get these bastards the ancestral way," she said with confidence.

OUR SPIRITUALITY

There's always been an altar, or what some people might call a shrine, at my house. My mom and dad would leave out our ancestors' favorite food and liquor, and would light candles weekly at the altar. They never forced me to participate as a kid, but our spirituality/religion was explained to me early in life, and I understood that my parents faithfully honor the spirits of the ancestors, and practiced their religion just like any other religion. When my dad suggested that my husband and I fly to New York for a special ritual, so we could make sure the right type of justice was handed to the killer cop, I was more than happy and willing to take part in it. Though I had to convince my husband at first, after explaining the process to him and schooling him a little more about the ceremony that took place at Bwa Kayiman during the Haitian revolution, he became more open-minded about participating. All the fake spooky details he had heard about Vodou was the figment of white people's imagination that infiltrated the minds of other people, including black people. The safest way to ensure that other members of my family avoided falling victim to violence, was to allow my dad to do what he knew best to protect the family.

My husband and I flew to New York, and planned for a five-day stay. Before leaving for New York, my father advised us not to tell anybody we were going, and it was best to turn off our phones during our stay in New York, which we did. We decided to stay at my parents' house because it helped facilitate everything smoothly. My parents prepped us for what was about to happen, but we really had no idea what to expect. My husband and I ate dinner with them the first night we got to New York. The next day, it was all about the ceremony that my dad planned, and we thought we were ready.

My dad organized a special religious Vodou ceremony with rituals that originated from the Vodum rooted in West and Central Africa, along with a couple of "Ougans" also known as Vodou priests, and a "Mambo" known as a Vodou priestesses. The ceremony was to celebrate our sons, and to invoke the Dahomian Lwa (spirits) of our ancestors to seek justice for the injustice that took the lives of our sons. The rituals of the ceremony consisted of a lot of drumming, dancing, music, singing, and possession of the body and mind by the lwa (spirits). All the initiates were dressed in white, as an identifier of their active participation in the religion, and also to reinforce the Rada rite of Dahomian ancestry. There were lit candles in a circle with other symbolic items that were necessary for the ceremony. I watched many people get possessed by the spirits, as if they were at a Baptist church, but these possession events felt real.

There was plenty of food. My dad bought a goat and a couple of chickens as part of the offerings to the ancestors. The three drummers were instrumental in heightening the spiritual energy in the room with their intensity on the beating drums. I could tell that my husband had never been to an event so riveting that he could almost feel the spirits overtaking him. My husband and I joined in the rhythmic dancing naturally, as if we were a part of the ceremony.

I'm not certain that I can explain all that went on, but I listened to a bunch of songs dedicated to each lwa, as the spirits are given their song and praise. The Ougans and the Manbos used their honed skills to wield their ason ak klochet (rattles and bells) to acknowledge and honor some spirits that were present in certain corners of the room. The center post also known as "potomitan" served as the anchor between the lwa, the altar, and the participants. There was a lot of what looked like well-choreographed dancing among the participants. My husband and I just fell into the rhythm as if we belonged. I want to say that these people had been around my dad, or at least had done these rituals with him for a long time, because they moved in unison, as if they had been performing these rituals for years. Along with the drummers, were, what looked like a synchronized choir, pounding the spirits into the bodies of the ceremony participants. There were a lot of head bows, rum, and water libations poured out to the dead, vaporizing gulps of rum into a mist over everyone, lit candles, and so much more. I was in awe, because it was actually the first time that I attended one of my dad's ceremonies as an adult. When I was younger, I was in the room without a care in the world, and didn't really pay much attention to what was going on. I expected my husband to feel uncomfortable because it was his first time at such an event, but somehow he felt right at home.

There many lwas (spirits) called upon during the ceremony, including Atibon Legba (the ancient one) who blesses everyone who bows before him, Marassa (the divine twins) are the playful ones who like candy, Danbala Wedo is the serpent lwa that usually writhes on the ground while covered with a white sheet by worshippers, Ezili Danto exudes power, pain, and strength, while tightly grasping daggers at each side, and so much more. Salutations around different parts of the room were abundant all night long. The ritual elements of Vodou are unique to each lwa. However, Ogou is the warrior spirit and he is special. I assume Ogou sits at the helm of all the spirits, because he was presented with a sword. I had never been in that mystical world, but from the moment the ceremony started around 9:00 PM, my husband and I felt right at home. We didn't realize it was early morning by the time everything ended. I wish I could give more details, but I can't remember it all. I didn't have time to pay attention to my in-laws and my husband's siblings who were also in attendance, but from what they told me, it was the most exhilarating experience for all of them.

The next day, my dad told us that everything necessary was done to get the results that were needed, for nature will take its course, as revenge will start taking shape without my husband lifting a finger. Trey and my cousin Big J.P were a little disappointed they weren't going to get a chance to let off a few slugs in this killer cop, but we were glad that they came down to support us and were ready to go to war alongside my husband. Going to New York is always a little reprieve from our daily routine, but this time around, I wasn't in the mood to act like a tourist with my husband around the city, so we stayed in at my parents' house until we flew back home four days later.

THE TRUTH
UNFOLDS

No sooner did we land in Atlanta, I noticed that my brother Jeff and my sister Cynthia had been blowing up my phone. I had turned my phone off while we were in New York, so they couldn't reach me. The minute the plane landed in Atlanta, I turned my phone back on, and I saw the alerts for almost twenty text messages and multiple voice messages. They also tried to reach my wife and left her multiple messages as well. I was hesitant to read the texts or listen to the messages, because I knew my siblings were in the trenches at the protests, and I didn't want to hear any bad news about them. My attorney also tried to reach me. In the span of a few days, what could've gone so wrong? I said to myself. I turned to my wife to say something, but she could see that look of worry on my face, before I even opened my mouth. "Everything's gonna be alright. Just have faith," she said, trying to comfort me. "We got this. I believe in the will of my ancestors, and I believe my father is doing everything in his power to protect our family," my wife followed. I looked at her and said, "I believe. I have faith, babe," as I moved my finger to scroll through my messages. The first message that I read stated, "Great news! Call me as soon as you can. Love you, big bro." It was a message from my brother Jeff. The second message I read said, "Call me, Big head. We have wonderful news for you. Love you." It was from my sister Cynthia. My parents always ingrained in our minds since we were children, to always remember to let each other know that we love one another because we are all that we got. My mind was a little bit at ease after reading the first message, so I didn't even bother reading the rest of the messages before I dialed Jeff's number to call him. I wanted to know what was so urgent.

As my wife and I got off the air-train to walk toward the escalators at Jackson International Airport to head toward baggage claim to retrieve our luggage, I felt a powerful trance of strength overcome me, while the phone rang in my ears, as I waited for my brother to pick up. My wife held my hand tightly and waited impatiently to hear what my brother had to say. Of course, Jeff didn't pick up. So, I called my sister, and she picked up right away. "Big bro, what's up? Have you heard the news?" she asked me. All I could hope for was some good news. "What news? I was in New York with Candace the last few days. What happened?" I asked. My sister got all excited on the phone and said, "Wait til you hear this! Ole boy had been targeting and abusing black people since he joined the police department, and his superiors never did anything about it. He had more complaints filed against him than the Department of Justice has filed against Trump. His record was buried, but your lawyer did a great job to subpoena his record and making it public. There are all types of allegations against this guy, and there's absolutely no way he will be able to keep his job, or avoid going to jail." I'm not sure if it's the best news that I had gotten lately, but it was better than I expected, and my faith in my ancestors' religion shot right up. My wife could tell that it was good news that I received from my sister, based on my facial expression alone. She turned to me and said, "Do you believe our spirituality is for real now?" as if she'd heard what my sister had just said to me. "I believe! I believe!" I replied. "Cynthia, hold on," I told my sister. "Babe, can we invite my brother and sister to the house tonight? Are you in the mood for company?" I asked her. "Why wouldn't I be in the mood to hear good news from my family? Of course, we can have them over," my wife told me. "Cynt, can you and Jeff come by the crib later, around 8 pm? By the way, I couldn't reach Jeff. If you talk to him before I do, let him know that we want to meet at the house tonight. Love you. Bye." Of course, she quickly reciprocated the affection and said bye.

My wife and I made our way to baggage claim, and as we waited for our luggage to appear on the carousel, we started reading the text messages together. It was all news about the discovery of Offi-

cer McNeal's blemished record at the police department since joining the force that they kept under wraps. We even saw the headline
on the big screen at the airport restaurant on CNN. A few of his
victims had decided to come forward to let the media know that
nothing had been done about the many complaints they had filed
against the killer cop, which led him to believe in his own invinci-
bility within the police department. More importantly, all his superiors, including his direct supervising sergeant, the lieutenant,
and the police captain, were all suspended by the police chief at his
station, after the revelation of McNeal's abuse history toward black
people and other minorities in Snellville, and because his superiors
did not follow protocol to resolve the multiple complaints that were
filed against a subordinate officer. All his misbehaving was pushed
under the rug because Officer McNeal was a legacy cop. His father
had worked for the police department in Snellville for 30 years, before retiring as a lieutenant. Nepotism runs deep throughout police
departments nationwide, and the Snellville Police Department is no
different. However, the problem lies in the fact that the blue line
of brotherhood is the depth of corruption throughout police departments across the nation, and most cops won't risk crossing that
line. The police work as an intimidating gang, and all the members
must abide by the gang's rules.

It's not so much that Officer McNeal's violations of people's
rights went unnoticed, but more about his daddy's legacy at the de-

partment that shielded him from discipline. Before the feds would be called in for an investigation, the police chief decided enough was enough, because he wasn't going to allow some silver spoon fed, spoiled, and racist brat, to tarnish the reputation of his department, as if he needed any help. McNeal was immediately suspended without pay for his past aggression against minority residents of the Snellville community, as well as the on-going investigation into his killings of my sons. Still, there was more icing on the cake to come, because a Latina woman whom McNeal arrested while she was a minor five years prior, also decided to come forward to speak about the sexual favors he requested from her, in order to let her go, in addition to the threats he made against her family, because they were Hispanic. She performed the illegal sexual acts as demanded by McNeal, but she also recorded the incident, and had been struggling emotionally ever since, because he had threatened to have her family deported, because of their illegal status, if she went to the authorities. McNeal knew of her family's status, because her name was on the DACA database. DACA is the Deferred Action for Childhood Arrivals program that was implemented by President Obama in 2012. There was a possibility that Officer McNeal was going to be charged with statutory rape, because the woman was only a 15-year-old minor at the time. The police chief didn't want all that drama associated with his police department.

In light of the revelations about all the illegal activities of Officer

McNeal, the city decided to expeditiously settle with my family for a record-setting 25 million dollars. My attorney had left me many messages to call him, and vaguely mentioned the city of Snellville's police department's settlement offer. My wife and I thought hard about the offer, and how we would be able to assist my brother and sister in their fight for justice, not just for our sons, but for all the victims of police brutality throughout the nation. While our original plan to establish a scholarship in the names of our sons, we also decided to help fund a nonprofit social justice group founded by my brother Jeff and my sister Cynthia called "No More." Jeff and Cynthia had mentioned their lofty goal of helping to fight police brutality against black people nationwide, but they were too ashamed to ask the public for funding, because of the history of Black Lives Matter's murky finances. We were more than happy to allocate at least 5 million dollars to their decentralized political and social foundation.

THE HEAT

Cynthia and Jeff managed to develop a following of people on social media, without officially having an organized group. It was a grassroots effort to bring different people together to help protest the death of my sons daily at police headquarters in Snellville. Without an official name, the media didn't know how to refer to the protesters who showed up daily at police headquarters in Snellville. However, they made it clear that they were not affiliated with Black Lives Matter in any shape or form. Actually, No More was born out of the death of my sons. My brother had long registered No More as a nonprofit entity seeking justice for victims of police abuse and brutality, but hadn't yet launched it. He sprung into action after the deaths of my sons, without even knowing where they were headed. It took a lot of effort on the part of the volunteers to keep the pressure on the police department to do something about the deaths of two innocent black boys, my sons. In addition, there was another group of black heavily-armed men, dressed in black, who also showed up at City Hall to demand justice for my sons every day, without ever revealing who they were. They never made any empty threats, they just demanded justice and made it clear that the city had better deliver justice, or there would be chaos in Snellville. The armed group of black men started out with just 50 black men carrying assault rifles and automatic weapons with heavy ammunition wrapped over their shoulders, reminiscent of the Black Panther Party of the sixties, but there was no identifier to dictate who they were. They simply dressed in all black and they were armed to the teeth. The group grew from 50 members on the first day of protest to over 500 members, when justice for my sons kept getting delayed. Of course, white people weren't exactly comfortable seeing a sea of armed black men in front of city hall and police headquarters every day. However, given the fact that Georgia is an open-carry state, there was nothing the police could do about it.

I never anticipated there would be a group of armed black men supporting our family's endeavor toward justice, but I secretly admired every single one of them. There was never any communication between what the mainstream media started referring to as "the black militia group" and them. They refuse to officially sit with the media to address their purpose, goal, or mission for the armed protest for my sons' deaths. Everything that they wanted to say to the world was written on the signs most of their members were carrying. When they were pushed to answer the question about leadership for the group by the associated press, every one of them stepped forward and in unison answered, "We are all leaders," confusing the hell out of the media. As usual, the media was trying to identify a target, so they could go back to their old blueprint of cutting off the head of the snake, by assassinating the leader of the group. There were no women in the group, however, by the 10th day of the protests, the armed group had grown to thousands of black people dressed in black and armed to the teeth. White people in Gwinnett County grew agitated and were afraid of what might transpire if the city didn't resolve this case as soon as possible. Transparency was the name of the game, and the mayor and police chief became as transparent as could be. Every day at 9:00 AM for two months straight, almost five thousand armed black people united and gathered in front of City Hall and police headquarters in Snellville.

This was the first time I had seen black people working together independently for one common goal, which was justice. My brother's group, No More, kept the pressure in the most diplomatic way, while the armed group of "Black Men in Black" was more demanding militantly. Of course, the mayor of Snellville reached out to me and my wife to ask us to quell the violence, but there was no violence. Everyone protested peacefully, but the Black Men in Black were intimidating and ready, in case the police wanted to bring it. My sons were murdered during the Covid19 epidemic, while many other black people were being urged to poison themselves with a jab. The epidemic worked favorably to the Black Men In Black because they were all wearing black masks. No one in the group could be identified by the police or any other law enforcement agency. It seemed as if they took all precautionary measures to make sure they couldn't be identified.

Black people all over the country were proud of these men who came together and risked their lives to seek justice for two little black boys who were murdered unjustifiably by a racist cop. The more the mainstream media dug into the group, the more inconspicuous and evasive they became. The one thing white people tend to lose their mind over, is not being able to control a situation. The Black Men in Black had done their homework regarding the nature of white people, and they used every tactic they studied to instill fear without ever saying a word to anybody. The police were the most cordial I had ever seen them, while they were facing the barrels of shotguns, AK-47s and AR-15s. There was no pushing or shoving of these men. Communication and interaction were humane and civil for the first time during a protest.

CAN'T HANDLE
THE HEAT

While pressure was being applied to the police department and the mayor's office, Officer McNeal's history of terrorist tactics against minority folks was being posted on social media daily, and words spread quickly that his arrest was imminent. The Georgia Bureau of Investigation determined that Officer Kevin McNeal was a rogue cop, and an arrest warrant would be issued. Meanwhile, my brother and sister were out there every day mobilizing as many people to police headquarters and city hall as possible. The group grew into thousands of people, outnumbering the police and the National Guards. No arrest was made, and everyone went home every day to live another day. My siblings led an organization that protected them and their members, because all the male members dressed In Black were armed,well-trained, ready and undeterred. Black people have to recognize they need to arm themselves to keep the police from infringing on their rights to protest. There's not one arrest recorded during the protests, and the organized protests yielded the best results and solutions we have ever seen, without any additional black lives lost. However, the situation was different for Officer Kevin McNeal, his sergeant, lieutenant, and captain. It turned out that the police precinct in Snellville was filled with rogue cops who were aided by the sergeant, lieutenant, and captain. The conspiracy to bury complaints filed against the department was set in place by the police captain, in order to keep the Snellville Police Department at the top of the chart of good policing and diversity. While it's true that Snellville is one of the most diverse cities in Gwinnett County, the leadership in Snellville does not represent its diversity. Black people make up over 50.8 percent of the population in Snellville, while the leadership at the top posts of the police department consists of 67 percent white people. That is not a good example of proper representation. In terms of black police officers hired by the city of Snellville, that information is buried where it can't be found, but pictures of police officers posted on the department's social media accounts only suggest that the number of black police officers working for that department is not on par with the demographics of the city of Snellville.

The false narrative surrounding the death of my sons shifted when the media could no longer find a way to uphold white privileges they have handed out to killer cops who have killed black people in the past, while crucifying the dead black victims posthumously. My sons were innocent children who were well-behaved, and were great example students at their school, and great citizens in their community. There was no blemish to find, but the media tried and alluded to many things that were untrue about them. The pressure for the media to do the investigative work to unearth the truth about Officer McNeal was mounting. However, before they could dig into Officer McNeal's background, he was found hung to death in his basement, with his hands tied behind his back, and his hanging was live on his Instagram account on his phone. The only information that is known about his death, is the fact that his hanging wasn't a suicide. There was no sign of forced entry at his house, and his tongue was also extracted from his mouth.

Whether it was divine intervention, or our prayers had been answered by the ancestors, we'll never know. I just know that I have more faith in my African spirituality than ever before. There's no way to prove vodou works, just like we haven't been able to prove the existence of Jesus Christ, or the idea of a heaven created by the enslavers to keep black folks in line. However, I knew that my in-laws had done a ceremony, and the goal was for us to find justice for our boys. How the justice came, doesn't really matter to my wife and me. I know my cousin Trey and Big J.P were long gone after the cop's body was found, because I spoke with them when they got to Boston and New York, and they both had alibis. Unfortunately, the two cops assigned to keep watch over Officer McNeal also didn't have much luck. They were found dead in their patrol cars with a bullet to the skull of each officer, across the street from the house. We just wanted justice, and if the ancestors had anything to do with it, we want to thank them for the great work they have done. Officer Kevin McNeal was no hero. He violated the rights of many members of the community, and no one was willing to put a stop to it, but more importantly, he was enabled by a system that has been supported by a government that refuses to abide by its own constitution that all men are created equal, and that life, liberty and the pursuit of happiness is a birthright for all Americans.

The ancestral justice didn't end with Officer McNeal. The spirits of the ancestors were hard at work, rooting out the corruption within the Snellville Police Department from top to bottom. The supervising sergeant of Officer McNeal was also found dead in the basement of his house. He was the main enforcer of the quota system for arrests at the police precinct in Snellville that targeted black people. The lieutenant and captain signed off on the quota practice, as well as the evidence tampering that took place at that station. Both, the lieutenant and captain, were forced to resign without receiving their full pension, as the Department of Justice threatened to do a thorough investigation into their handling of cases at the precinct, since they've been in their leadership positions. It was easier for the lieutenant and captain to resign because they were going to face corruption charges and a long prison sentence. Once again, the work of the ancestors was nothing short of miraculous. There's more than one way to get justice or results, but black people have turned their backs and forgotten their own God, to worship a deity that was beaten into the minds, body and soul of their ancestors. Supposedly, God is a jealous God, right? Why would your God take you out of your misery, when you don't even want to acknowledge His existence? Black people continue to worship and acknowledge a God that was fabricated for them, and who has not punished the people who have enslaved their ancestors, and continue to marginalize and subjugate them, a God who has forced poverty as a religion upon them globally, while they continue to justify their own maltreatment with a bible that was handed to them to punish them, force them into submission for slavery, and commit them to a life of poverty. I've become so enlightened since I've met my wife. I don't know what I would do without her.

Black people have been under siege and living under a microscope of injustice from the day the first ship arrived on African shores to gather illegal cargo of humans in the 1600s. The inventors of human trafficking from Europe and America found a way to make slavery legal globally, without ever being protested by the so-called "good white people" of the world in an international court of law. When descendants of formerly forcefully enslaved people in the Caribbean, South America, Brazil, and America bring up the topic of reparations, the conversion of global hatred takes precedence over the humane reality that the wrongs of their forefathers must be righted. Atonement is not a word that too many white people are privy to, because it's the antonym of white privilege. Financial reparations to black people globally would more than likely wipe out poverty in many countries across Africa, the Caribbean, and America for black folks. White superiority is based on a false sense of themselves they created to pacify their ego and fragility. The first world status of countries across Europe and America was developed off the hard work of formerly enslaved Africans, because these folks lacked the ingenuity, the work ethic, the resilience, and the determination to create their own developed world. Black labor is the backbone of the world's economy.

My awakened journey has allowed me to use a different set of eyes, whenever I see white people now. There's nothing humane about their history in the world. America alone has invaded 84 out of 193 countries in the world, and for the most absurd reasons. Most of the time, it was to gain control of resources of the countries they invaded, so they could turn around and tell the world how poor these countries are. It's funny enough that the American government acts as if they are the biggest philanthropists around the world, while they are indebted to the entire world simultaneously. America owes a combined total of 32 trillion dollars to many countries around the world, including countries they refer to as third-world, like the Bahamas that they owe billions to. One of the main reasons they feel they can be in debt for so much money, is because the US government doesn't plan on paying its debt, especially to countries that lack the military might to go to war with them. The US government is the personification of gangster. Out of 193 countries in the world, the US government has been involved militarily with 191 of them. That is a 98% involvement rate. This country breeds war and destruction, but they're quick to point to black-on-black crime in America to disavow the misdeeds of white people in the world.

It's unfortunate that black people, not just in America, but across Africa and the Caribbean, where they were colonized, and subjected to the criminal behaviors of these savages who set out to rule the world, don't take heed of that history. Criminal behavior is learned behavior and Europeans have played a major role in teaching criminality to black folks around the globe. No other group on this planet has killed more people around the world than white people. It's as if their endless thirst for destruction can never be quenched. They are the original terrorists of the world. World War III is looming, and all the "first world/superpower" countries can't wait to show the world how easily they can annihilate each other, with their endless attempts to create biological, chemical, radiological warfare, and of course, the old and favorite one, nuclear weapons. It is a mental and psychological illness to want to end the world and kill all the people in it. If their goal is to destroy humanity and start over after emerging from their underground bunkers with their immediate family members, I feel sorry for them, because they are the sorriest, psychologically demented, sociopathic, and mentally disturbed despicable scum of the earth.

Slavery, as it appears now, was just the tip of the iceberg. I question whether these people are actually human all the time. Millions of innocent people have been killed worldwide by these so-called leaders of the world, and none of them have yet to see the interior of a prison cell for crimes against humanity. Many leaders have been assassinated by the US government, and no international court has ever challenged American tyranny. In short, they, along with their European allies, have managed to turn most of the countries in the world into plantations that they can control and destroy at will. I wish I never started down this path to learn about true US history, slavery, and the marginalization of all people by the one percent, because now I can't stop thinking about it. The only thing I can do for now, is try my best to protect my family and reconnect with my African roots. I'm grateful for my wife and her family, because they've shown me the power of our own spirituality, and to be proud of my African heritage. No matter how much these colonizers have imposed this self-hatred on us through psychological undermining tactics, we can never get away from who we truly are as a people. Our will can never be broken, because we are a resilient people by nature. They don't know how to handle that. Being of African descent is a privilege. We are the true Gods of the earth. Hopefully, one day all black people will embrace that truth!

FAMILY FIRST

I believe that I'm the luckiest woman in the world, in spite of what happened to my two sons. Of course, there's no joy in losing my twin boys at the hands of an overzealous scumbag in a uniform with a gun and badge, who had no respect for human life, but I became lucky when I married a man who truly epitomizes the true definition of a husband, father, son, brother, cousin, and family man. My husband is also the epitome of strength. I don't know what I would've done without my husband and the support of my family. Being an emotional wreck is not even half of it. I had no idea how I was going to get through this tragedy. My sons had become an integral part of my life, and I didn't know the first thing about dealing with the pain of losing, not one, but two sons, at the same time. I had to pull myself together, and with the assistance of my husband, I managed to confront my fears, overcome my pains, dealt with my emotions, as it related to the loss of my children. I'm still a work in progress, but my husband has been my rock and my strength. I just hope that I bring the same balance, peace of mind and strength that he needs in his life as well, because I've never met anybody emotionally stronger and more disciplined than my husband. Sometimes I wake up fearing that my husband may not make it back home, but I'm also aware that his mindset is totally different now, especially after the deaths of our sons, and there's no way in hell he's going to allow himself, or his family, to be a victim of the system again.

This tragedy has brought my entire family full circle. It's been a journey of self-discovery for many of us. Partially due to my husband's military background and his experience with tours in Iraq and Afghanistan, the family, and I'm sure even the police, expected him to become the next Chris Dorner, because he had so much love for his sons. He adored those boys and would give up his own life for them. However, my husband is also very cerebral, which is why I married him. Still, I didn't realize he came from a family of critical thinkers, until I learned some of the most unlikely heroes in this tragedy never had any military experience at all. Everyone knows my husband is not irrational in any way, but losing your children can drive you mad. As his wife, I was hoping it never got to the point where my husband would be driven to madness. I'm certain that my husband woke up every day and thought of the most destructive ways to exact revenge on the entire police department, not just the killer cop, for the deaths of our sons, while shielding me from his plan at the same time. I was worried every day of what he might do. He's the quiet type, and those people are the most dangerous when faced with obstacles and adversities beyond their control. However, it was his brother, Jeff, and his sister Cynthia, who planned, plotted, and organized the destruction of this cop publicly. Of course, my husband played a major role by digging into the killer cop's background, but it was his siblings who orchestrated the takedown of the police department from the very beginning. I'm gonna go ahead and give credit to the ancestors as well, because my father was adamant we needed to call on the ancestors for justice. I'm glad it all worked out.

It turned out that Jeff and Cynthia weren't just activists, they had been well-trained members of a black militia in Georgia for years, without ever revealing it to their immediate family. They had been in the trenches for years, but were galvanized into action quicker than anticipated, because the victims were their nephews. I'm just happy their plan to avenge the deaths of their nephews in the most devastating way, didn't come to fruition. Apparently, Cynthia and Jeff had had enough of the senseless killing of black people by police around the country, so they formed an underground militia to fight police corruption when and wherever it was necessary. You can call them our secret agents, if you will. While Cynthia acted as spokesperson for the group, "No More," during the process of the protests, Jeff was the minister of information, planner, and leader of the entire movement. No More was the front part of the group, and the diplomatic branch, while the militants who dressed in all black were the actual enforcers and battle-ready soldiers who swore to uphold the mission statement established by the group, and took an oath with their lives. The activist group, No More's mission statement to seek justice wherever injustice exists, was very different than the secret oath the members took to murder every killer cop for every member of the black community that is murdered unjustly by the police. Every member of the group is required to train for six months, which included physical and mental training, combat training, weapons and ammunition training, as well as self-discipline training. Jeff and Cynthia had undergone all those trainings, without any members of the family knowing.

The protests were strategically organized, and nobody knew that the "Armed Black Men In Black" and the regular protesters were part of the same group, No More. The protesters who appeared like normal civilian protesters were also armed every day when they showed up to protest, as it was a requirement. The goal of the group is to end police tyranny by instilling the same fear in them that they have managed to instill into black people's minds and hearts. Of course, upon learning this at a family function, my first question was, "Where do I sign up?" My husband and I both became members, and we fight to seek justice for innocent victims of police brutality across the country. The 25-million-dollar settlement we received from the city of Snellville and Gwinnett County came in handy, as it has allowed us to help finance the group and recruit members across the country. We are still an underground group. The lawyer who represented us against the city was so impressed with the "Armed Men In Black," we couldn't keep the movement a secret from him. He decided to become a member as well and waived his fee for representation, to help finance the group. Our members come from all walks of life. Some of them are judges, CEO's, teachers, nurses, firefighters, and regular plain folks.

Things are looking up, because change is gonna come. I'm very appreciative that my husband's family has decided to embrace my culture. At first, there might've been resistance and a little bit of ignorance, due to the false narrative about Haiti, Haitian culture, and the livelihood of Haitians living in Haiti by the US media, but we've weathered the storm and persevered as a family. We've managed to learn to keep an open mind toward black culture overall, not just African-American culture or Haitian culture, but the entirety of African culture, because we understand that wherever they dropped off our ancestors as captives during the Atlantic Slave trade, does not remove our African heritage. The different languages, religions, customs, and last names they have forced upon us as a stolen people, is not our true identity. We teach our children that black unification is a must. The devil has never taken a day off, and neither should we. We must do everything in power now to unify, in order to destroy an enemy that is far-reaching, and so well-organized, only group economics and African unity can destroy them.

As a couple and parents, we are still grieving the deaths of our sons, but my husband has done everything in his power to make sure that things never fall apart in our household. I want to be there for him, because I can feel his strength, but I can't really cope as well as him just yet. At night, we talk about our feelings and some-times shed tears for our boys together, but I know watching tears fall out of the corner of my husband's eyes every time we talk about our boys, is only a sign of his strength. For now, we are closer than ever, our bond, our love and dedication to each other can never be deterred or disturbed by any outside forces.

Meanwhile, my husband and I were excited when a pregnancy test confirmed that we were pregnant once again. Things would get even better after a visit to the office of my black gynecologist who told us to be prepared once again to care for a new set of fraternal twins, a boy and a girl. I can't describe the feelings that came over me, after learning we were pregnant. Our entire family was excited by the news, but this time, things will be very different. History will never repeat itself!

THE GODS OF
THE EARTH?

It was fascinating to hear that the so-called "Karen" who made the initial call to the police, to report the danger and threat my sons posed to the park visitors, which ultimately ended in the deaths of our sons, was found dead in her bathtub at home due to a drug overdose. The syringe filled with the deadly substance to give her a temporary escape was still stuck on her arm, when her body was discovered. We don't know if it was a mystical act from our ancestors who heard our prayers, or if Trey and Big J.P decided to play executioners on our behalf. However, they had more than enough information on how to find her, because I provided it to them. At least there's one less Karen in the world who will have the opportunity to call the police on innocent black boys for no reason. Whether a person chooses to believe in God or not, it shouldn't really matter to the rest of us, because a lot of "Godly" people in the world are committing the most heinous crimes, from statutory rape to murder. However, everyone should question why white people think they are in a position to play God on earth. They want to change everything that nature has created, including the weather, our naturally grown food, people's natural sex, and the list is endless. Their appetite for destruction is ungodly, unless the God they serve is a destructive manifested through them? They have an affinity to stay youthful and live infinitely. They also want to dictate how many people have the right to live on this Earth and how many should die, in order to make room for the ones they believe have more rights to life than others. They want to murder world leaders who disagree with them at will, and are forever creating weapons of mass destruction to end the world.

While most white people act like they adhere to the fictitious teachings of the bible they used to enslave Africans, in order to appear pure, there's nothing about them that dictates purity, peace and serenity. Did they really come up with the actual Ten Commandments in the bible? They have used the Commandments to tame and control the world. The United States government is one of the greatest violator of the Ten Commandments daily. America prides itself as a Christian country, but what is so Christian about America? Christian values seem to be based on everything that is pro-white and against everybody else. America's false propaganda of high morals has spread around the world like wildfires. The notion that basic Human Rights are afforded to all people in this country is just that, a notion and a right reserved for white people, not just in America, but across the world. Still, white people can't stop acting like they're the gods of the earth.

Why must black people continue to depend on affirmations and social movements to reinforce our sense of beauty (Black is beautiful), our sense of being (We have Right to live and be), our survival (Black Lives Matter), and everything else that encompasses black life? It's because America doesn't know how to remove herself from her racist roots. We preach one thing to the world, while practicing something entirely different against those citizens who were once deemed to be three fifths human under a constitution that proclaims all men are created equal. That double talk has allowed racism to thrive in America under the watchful eyes of the world. I laid my life on the line to defend a country that refuses to allow me to assert my basic human rights, while they're pointing fingers to every corner of the world they've poached, with human rights violations. America is the biggest supporter of slave labor in the world, which is why most US companies have outsourced their manufacturing to countries where people live below the poverty line, and are paid slave wages that only benefit the American companies.

It's not a coincidence that we are still fighting for the same basic human rights that Dr. King, Malcolm X, Fred Hampton, Patrice Lumumba, Kwame Nkrumah, and many other black leaders have lost their lives over. America refuses to acknowledge her racist past, thus racism continues to thrive in a fake melting pot and ideals that America has sold, and continues to sell to the world. My sons should be alive today, if America lived up to her promises that all men are created equal, and everyone should have a right to liberty and the pursuit of happiness. My sons were underage children who were being raised in a hostile environment they didn't understand or were aware of, and the hostility was limited to their skin color. How long is America going to keep up this hostility against black people? Their history dictates that the hostility began with them, the rapes began with them, the kidnappings began with them, the murders began with them, the invasions begin with them, the terror began with them, and the theft of resources began with them, the kidnappings begin with them. Black people in America, and the West, overall, have been duped, brainwashed, and forced to believe they are their own worst enemy, and the worse enemy of the world. Until a great awakening takes place with our people, we're going to continue to live under the auspicious belief that strides have been made to end white imperialism. Unfortunately, my sons will not be the last victims of the pervasive racism practiced by the police across America. Hopefully, black America will start to wake up, and they will start taking the marginal steps to change things for the next generation, because all these peaceful marches have only added to the callous on our feet, and are nothing but fundraisers for the police departments. Peaceful protesters are often arrested, charged, and indicted. The only groups that benefit from that are the police, the jail system, the courts, and the justice department.

RICHARD JEANTY

True freedom is not free. True freedom is not docile. True freedom is not submissive. True freedom is not passive. True freedom is not nonviolent. True freedom is not peaceful. True freedom requires bloodshed.

Made in the USA
Columbia, SC
27 January 2024